Senseless Women

Senseless Women

STORIES

Sarah
Harris
Wallman

UNIVERSITY OF MASSACHUSETTS PRESS
Amherst and Boston

ISBN 978-1-62534-518-9 (paper)
Designed by Sally Nichols
Set in Scala and Lumios Marker
Printed and bound by Maple Press, Inc.

Cover design by TG Design, Inc.
Cover photo by H. Armstrong Roberts, *1940s blond girl wearing blindfold arms up
in air feeling reaching*, May 4, 1945. Colorized by Trudi Gershenov.
ClassicStock/Alamy Stock Photo E8T447

Library of Congress Cataloging-in-Publication Data

Names: Wallman, Sarah Harris, author.
Title: Senseless women / Sarah Harris Wallman.
Description: Amherst ; Boston : University of Massachusetts Press, [2020] |
Series: Juniper prize for fiction
Identifiers: LCCN 2019044404 | ISBN 9781625345189 (paperback) | ISBN
9781613767689 (ebook) | ISBN 9781613767696 (ebook)
Classification: LCC PS3623.A44523 A6 2020 | DDC 813/.6—dc23
LC record available at https://lccn.loc.gov/2019044404

British Library Cataloguing-in-Publication Data
A catalog record for this book is available from the British Library.

Contents

Senseless Women

The Dead Girls Show

Carly had been going to the Dead Girls Show since she was twelve. The little theater was wedged between Live Girls and Girls Girls Girls, a block down from the city's least expensive dentist. She went at least twice a year to both, entering the show with a nice painkiller buzz that was gradually replaced by a feeling like biting a cement candy bar.

The place had been a movie theater; it smelled of popcorn and feet and still ran a sparsely stocked concession stand. There was only one other person in the seats, a man in a puffy coat. She settled in a few rows ahead of him with a paper cup of ice cream, peeled the lid, and went at it with a little wooden paddle.

Arabella was first: the anorexic. In the greeny spotlight, she looked like a starved mermaid. She stared upward as if pleading with the spotlight man for a respite that never came. As her pedestal began to rotate, her eyes stayed fixed on the booth even as her body turned away. The spot ignited the downy arm hair her fatless body had sprouted as a last defense against the cold. When the pedestal had completed its rotation, Arabella rose to her feet and continued staring out as an elfin figure in a top hat and tails came onto the stage with a bucket of colored water. The little man (though Carly knew it was a girl, one of the trio who cleared the stage between acts) poured the water and dye over Arabella's shoulders so the audience could see how it pooled in her clavicle and traced the contours of her bulging knees. Her droopy bikini was so soaked that the bottoms fell heavily to her ankles with a small splash. Her pubic hair was sparse and red.

Somewhere behind the seats a machine whirred, and then, projected on scrim, were poems the girl had written about despair. The recorded voice that accompanied them was a smoker, a man. For an extra fee, you could go with Arabella into a back room where she served you tea and described how her stepfather groped her.

For her finale, Arabella arched her back and spread her arms. Her eyes were exquisite with the knowledge of suffering. The girl in the top hat yanked out the halter knot and the bikini top tumbled down to the floor with the bottom. Her breasts lay against her ribs like baby mice in a pair of socks.

Not all of them used names. Next is the Ballerina, wearing only the skirt of a tutu. One of her ankles is crumbled and loose, but she shows it no mercy as she pirouettes and lunges about to a Chopin mazurka that becomes increasingly frantic and demented. She reaches out her lovely arms as if for a rescuer.

Carly has nothing in common with these girls, but her heart leaps with them. Her limbs, on the other hand, are more generously padded. Her elbow is more like a dimple than a spear. Her feet in sensible shoes like loaves of bread.

Regina, the drowned girl, is wheeled out in her tank. Her eyes are open, but without pupils they look like giant pearls set in the prongs of her eyelashes. Her lips move so that she seems to say *please, please, please,* but the only sound is the delicate bloop of three bubbles that escape from her mouth. Three silver bubbles, then no more.

When she is gone the three stagehands scurry to mop up the mossy-smelling water that has sloshed onto the floor. They are not elves or even dwarfs; they are girls who died very young of cancer, bald and delicate and—perhaps as a side effect of some experimental drug—pointy about the ears.

A strobe light begins to pulse, but without music. The Hanged Girl comes out wearing a Catholic school uniform complete with red tie. The pale purple of her face is smeared with black eyeliner, liberally applied and liberally tear-streaked. Anyone who has been to the show before knows that her arms are ribboned with cuts, but that day she wears a bulky starter jacket in a Carolina blue. "Panthers." It ruins the effect, Carly thinks. What girl would kill herself after receiving a team captain's jacket?

The man two rows behind agrees: "Take it off!"

The Hanged Girl, who usually keeps her head bobbing loose around her chest and shoulders, suddenly straightens. "No, thank you."

Carly hears a nylon swizz that must be the guy in the puffy jacket standing. "Fuck you!" he yells. He has to be a regular: in regular shows, the Hanged Girl comes out to a Metallica song and screams *fuck you* at the audience, her middle fingers a staccato jab in the strobe light. It's very dramatic.

This time she only shrugs. "I'm not doing that anymore."

A jumbo slurpee hurtles over Carly's head and splatters on the stage. The Hanged Girl spreads the slush around with the toe of her black Converse, lights a cigarette, walks off.

Carly hears the heckler's sticky steps, then muffled shouting from the lobby.

There is a pause in the action. Carly digs for a piece of gum, but in the flashing light the contents of her large purse are garish and elusive. Finally, the strobe goes off and a pink glow suffuses the room. They are skipping the prom-night car crash victim and going straight to the grand finale.

The pink is bright enough to illuminate Carly's flattened pack of Juicy Fruit and a few unseemly stains on the seats around her.

The stagehands push Meghan, the serial rapist/killer's victim, onto the stage. Meghan is really just a pile of limbs in a wheelbarrow with a head propped on top, but her voice is deep and commanding. She doesn't have her own act, but always introduces the last one.

"Ladies and gentleman," Meghan's mouth projects especially well, having been widened several inches by her assailant's knife, "it is said that unicorns walk the earth. Most of us will never see them. For so the legend has it that only the purest virgin can capture a unicorn . . ."

The sprite pushing Meghan's wheelbarrow quickly rearranges one of the dismembered arms so that it gestures stage left.

Electronic birdsong fills the theater and Carly begins to tear up. In the hazy moments after her own lost virginity, Carly had thought not of the bare mattress beneath her or the bikini model affixed to the ceiling above her, but the fact that unicorns were now officially beyond her.

The birdsong increases in volume and is joined by the chirp of rusty wheels as the unicorn slowly begins to emerge. It is, of course, a stuffed horse altered by some whimsical taxidermist of a prior decade. For several long seconds, the audience sees only the head with its purple glass eye; then, in a crescendo of computerized mockingbird, the unicorn's rider appears: astride the moth-eaten flanks is little Adrianna, still in her satin sash and sequined tiara. The froth of yellow dress is ripped in a few places and, like a tiny Cinderella, she is missing her left shoe. As the wheeled unicorn rotates, the audience sees that on her right side, her frilly sock is brown with old blood; a runnel of crusty brick runs from the sock up her leg, which is still faintly chubby.

The little queen smiles bravely, her glossy lips trembling. An obedient child, eager to please. She holds onto the saddle with one hand; the other reaches out to pet the unicorn's mane. A hank of hair tangles in her fingers and falls out, but she continues to stroke as if the horse, which for years has remained successfully dead, is in need of soothing.

Carly is crying fiercely now, nothing like the sparkling hints of water in Adrianna's jewel-blue eyes. Carly's face puffs out when she cries. Uneven splotches the pink of digestive aids cover her forehead and cheeks. There is nowhere for the tears to pool, so they run along her jaw and drop from her chin like a beard.

When she has recovered herself a bit, Carly stands to leave. In the lobby, the heckler argues with the tickets girl, who is not dead, just an ordinary sophomore with an after-school job.

"Look," says the girl, whose nose and eyes crowd the middle of her face as if shrinking from her acne, "you want to speak to him, fine. I give up. I'll get fired for this, but follow me."

Outside, Carly blinks in the sunlight. Her eyes are salted with tears and she tries to adjust them by focusing on the kicking neon leg of Girls Girls Girls. She does not see or hear the theater manager's car as he speeds out of the alley to avoid confrontation with the angry customer.

When he hits her, there is a sound like a water balloon finding its target.

Carly's last word is "Unk."

⚘

When Carly woke up, she was on the floor of the room behind the stage, her dislodged organs resting against the inside of her back. Her injuries, though fatal, were largely internal. Above her: rafters, pipes, and clotheslines hung with wet leotards, one of them dripping on her face. She realized she should flinch.

"What are we supposed to do with her, Milo?" The voice belonged to Karen, stage name the Hanged Girl.

Milo was a short, goateed man in glasses with purple lenses. He seemed too fidgety to answer.

"Maybe we can say she died in childbirth," said Arabella, "She's fat enough."

"She's not that fat. She's just *normal*." Karen turned the word sour, not a compliment.

"It was a split-second decision," said Milo, "I thought if the police showed up it would help for her to be speaking. You can, speak, can't you? I haven't resurrected another mute?"

"I can speak," said Carly, surprised that she could, actually. Her voice sounded a little rusty, but then it often did. Her days had never been terribly interactive.

"Who knows," said Milo, standing up a bit straighter, "I may need to start bringing in new performers."

"Empty threats, Milo. *That* could never replace me." Karen opened her button-down to reveal breasts that were perfectly formed and uniformly defaced with small black razorblade slashes.

"Those don't do me a lot of good offstage," Milo sniffed. "Now, miss, excuse me, but will anyone be missing you?"

Carly had to admit that no one would. Her manager would be mildly annoyed that no one on the late shift had been through the yogurts to check expiration dates, but people quit Stop & Shop without notice all the time. It was no cause for alarm.

"In that case, I shall take my nap." As Milo left, he clapped his hands twice. The three cancer girls sprang to his side and followed him out of the room. Up close, Carly could see that their ears were not pointed; they had been pinched and stitched at the top.

She looked around to see if anyone had noticed: there was little Adrianna, smoking a cigarette longer than her hand.

"Don't worry," scoffed the beauty queen, flicking ash. "Nothing hurts. Nothing causes cancer."

⤞

Nights backstage were long. Sleep was distasteful and unnecessary, so there was nothing to do but talk all night. The girls showed no interest in Carly's potential as an act, but when they found out she was a fan they were eager to hear about their own performances. What had Arabella's poetry meant to her? Did the Drowned Girl bloop enough bubbles? Was it really, really, unbelievably sad when Adrianna pet the unicorn?

"I hate that part," said Adrianna. "It's so cheesy."

"It always makes me cry," Carly confessed.

"Ew. Then why do you come?"

Karen answered for her: "She's a sap."

Carly tried to describe what the show had meant to her in middle school when she had the figure of a teddy bear, when she would go entire days without attracting the notice of anyone, not even her teachers, and the sight of Arabella in the spotlight made her nearly swoon with anticipation of all that might lie ahead: willowy arms, sad poems, pubic hair.

She tried to tell them about the times she and her high school boyfriend, who later turned out to be gay, would cut class and catch a matinee. They held hands through the whole thing, communicating in damp squeezes how moved they were by the Drowned Girl, the princess. He did sometimes snicker at Willa, the girl who died in a drunk-driving accident on the way home from the prom, and that, Carly thought, was a sign of why they would one day have to break up, eventually, when they went to college and were a little less lonely. She took in stride his justification for not kissing her with an open mouth: after all, the Milk Duds did stick in her braces.

The dead girls weren't interested in her life story. "Why did he laugh?" demanded Willa. She didn't have enough contiguous bones to stand, and when she wasn't being marionetted about the stage in her bloody strapless, she hung from a collapsible wooden rack for drying laundry.

Carly apologized: "He thought you must have been well liked. He thought anyone who was well liked must be a bad person."

When Carly finally got up the nerve to ask them what went on in their private shows, they laughed at her prurience. They couldn't have sex if they wanted to. Their insides were stuffed with sawdust. Hadn't Carly noticed?

She hadn't. Carly, always a slave to a hyperactive bladder, had rather enjoyed the respite from her old life, in which she always had to know where the next toilet might be hiding. Now, when she pulled down her underwear, she did see that a few loose shavings had settled there. And there was a vague piney taste at the back of her throat; it was not just that she had spent too much time around cleaners.

For she was cleaning now. As a car crash victim, she could not compare to Willa and she felt a need to be useful in some way. So she'd retrieved a cart of cleaning supplies from Milo's closet and was gradually trying to restore some sheen to the theater's dusty cataracts. In time, the girls trusted her to check their bodies' blind pouches for termites and in this way she came to know who they really were. They hid things. Change, mostly. They were mad for coins, though with nowhere to spend their money they carried it between their legs until it jingled out and was snatched up by another. Karen kept an airplane bottle of rum in her throat. The Ballerina had a small silver shoe from a Monopoly game in one ear, a pearl-tipped corsage pin in the other.

꜀

In her previous life, Carly's few moments of boldness (a karaoke song about her determination to survive, an afternoon in a bikini on a Cancun beach) were inflected with rum, and for this reason she sometimes hesitated before fitting the little bottle back into Karen's throat.

"Don't think about it," said Karen, "I mean, even if I didn't beat you up first, it would just get down in you and smell bad and Milo would have to replace your stuffing. He hates that."

"I wasn't thinking of anything," said Carly. "Not really." She held up the letterman jacket for Karen to climb back into. Karen had reached some kind of agreement with Milo whereby she no longer wore it on stage, but otherwise it left her shoulders only when Carly Windexed her armpits.

"Hey," said Karen, "buck up. I'll let you in on something."

"Okay," said Carly, a Christmas Eve eagerness breaking out on her face.

"Shh. Listen: don't take out the garbage until later. Like, after midnight. I'll meet you at the back door."

The hours after midnight were unpoliced: Milo slept on the futon in his office, guarded by his homemade pixies. The occasional howl or bottle breaking in the streets was adequate security: though they would never have admitted it, the girls were afraid of the world outside the theater. There was a rumor, which for some had converted into fixed belief, that fresher air would lead to swifter decay.

Still, Carly and her bag of theater trash followed Karen through the back door, propping it with a broken chair reserved for that purpose. Usually, Carly scrambled the five or six steps to the dumpster, heaved and lobbed the trash, then ran back to the door without waiting to hear it land, but that night Karen motioned for her to set it down as quietly as possible.

"There," she whispered, pointing deeper into the alley, "the tall one is Gary."

Three middle-aged men in Patriots caps stood with their shoulders back, urinating on the rear wall of the alley. Steam rose in the cold. Karen suppressed a giggle; Carly thought that since the night air did not hurt them that perhaps tomorrow she would give the area a good hosing off.

The urination took some time: clearly, the men had taken in prodigious amounts of fluid. At last, the sound of liquid hitting brick became intermittent and died out. The men shook themselves off and exchanged congratulatory murmurs.

"You guys must've drunk down an ocean," laughed Karen. They jumped, and she laughed again, "So, whadja bring me?"

The fear in the men's faces was only temporary: they exchanged smiles and came a little closer, searching their pockets. One had half a piece of gum in a shiny wrapper. The other held out a string bracelet of colored knots. The one called Gary presented Karen with the prize: a Canadian nickel, on one side an industrious beaver, on the other a queen in profile. Carly and Karen took turns holding the items, marveling at the left-over warmth that pulsed from each.

"You wanna dance?" said Gary. His grin floated unsteadily between chin and reddish nose. Men like this had often come into the grocery store in the wee hours. Usually, they staggered to the chips aisle and stood there for a long time, taking in the enormity.

Karen looked at him like he was a piping hot bowl of food. "Let's go!"

And just like that, she was dragging Carly to a curled-back

place in the chain-link fence that separated them from the concrete yard where Live Girls stored their trash. "When Gary was in high school, he was a quarterback for a team that won their region," Karen whispered as they ducked beneath.

"Panthers?"

"Yes!" Karen wrapped herself more tightly in the jacket. "He just *gave* me this!"

The club next door leaked a fuzzy red beer-sign light and thumping music. Karen immediately raised her arms and began to twist and untwist her hips. The men hooted appreciatively. Gary arranged himself behind her and bounced arhythmically at the knees. Karen flattened her back against him and slid toward the ground, then suddenly bounced up and pushed him playfully away.

"Carrr-leeee, come dance with me," she purred.

Carly did not want to say she didn't know how. After all, this type of music was fairly insistent: the only dance move it really suggested was a repetitive thrusting of the pelvis. She smiled weakly and began, just barely, to move her hips. Her lifted hands formed loose fists in front of her and she jiggled them, sarcastically at first. This was the only way she had ever danced, the way one danced at the periphery, rolling one's eyes with the other people who'd been shunted aside by the energy of the dance floor.

But Karen had transformed into the sort of figure you saw at the molten center of the dancers, her mouth tensed in a silent shout, her neck loose, her muscles electric. She straddled Carly's leg and began to bat it from one thigh to the other. She leaned in very close, her face angled so that their foreheads almost touched and her eyes were looking up into Carly's like a bull about to charge. Carly's fingers uncurled; her hands were suddenly on Karen's shoulders. The men were cheering, and yet the men were not really a part of it. The music, a song about women with booties who really needed it, needed it on the flo, was a part of them. When it shouted repeatedly for them to get on the flo, get on the flo, their thighs contracted like hydraulics, lower and lower. Carly didn't have long hair, but what she had she tossed back and forth like a shaken doll. They had lowered their rears within inches of the broken glass and concrete beneath them, but their legs held them and they would not be cut.

And then someone opened a window: the music poured out louder than before, along with a horsey smell of real sweat, live-girl sweat, so warm it brought Carly and Karen to their feet.

"Hey! What's going on back there?"

"We're busted!" Karen shrieked with delight, "Go!"

She grabbed Carly's hand and they ran back toward the theater, blowing kisses and shouting good-byes to Gary and his friends. They ran through the backstage area and up the aisles, all the way to the lobby, where they fell down laughing and grabbing at each other's arms.

Then Karen paused and frowned. She looked in danger of falling out of the moment: "Now what do we do?"

"I know a game," said Carly, "The boys in the stockroom used to play it . . . watch." She dug frantically through the concession-stand cabinets until she found what she wanted: square envelopes of instant hot chocolate. "What you do is, you pile as much as you can on a spoon, and see if you can swallow it. Whoever gets the most down wins." Carly bit her lip, worried that the idea would not appeal.

"I'll go first!" said Karen.

Soon they were coughing great clouds of powdered chocolate from their mouths and noses, every laugh causing a new eruption. The dusty air of the lobby took on a decidedly cocoa scent. Particles hung in a haze that dimmed the glow of the Pepsi logo on the soda fountain.

Then Karen said the thing that ruined it all: "Someday I'm just going to burn this whole place down."

"Why would you do that?"

"I don't know. Don't you hate it? Don't you just hate the whole thing?"

Actually, Carly had been thinking that she had never had a night as fun as this. "Okay," she said. "Let's wait though. I don't feel like burning it down tonight."

⚘

The next show was scheduled for 3:30 the following afternoon.

There was a small crowd outside the door before the first popped kernel had made its way over the rim of the popper. When the sophomore (that was the only way any of them ever referred to her) at last turned the locks (having already dirtied several rags trying to mop up the cocoa), they all piled in. One was a regular named Smoky. The rest were leggy women in short skirts and an assortment of cheap jackets. Some of them were smoking, and they did not stop when they entered the lobby. They formed a loose phalanx with a blonde at the front.

"There's no popcorn yet," said the sophomore, helpless and skinny in her greasy uniform, which was really only a sort of polyester bib that tied at the sides.

"Where are the gur-rills?" demanded the leader. Her nose was hooked in such a way that she seemed able to regard her adversary only by turning it one way or the other, then peering out from behind it with a single beady eye. She wore a coat made from the pelts of small creatures as helpless as the sophomore, but she wore it with a great personal dignity.

"We haf beez-niss with your gur-rills," she snarled.

Some of the other tall women looked like they might not have accents, but none of them spoke. They all glared impassively; some had their heads tilted practically horizontal with attitude.

"The show doesn't start for another half hour."

"We do not weesh to see this show," the leader tossed the nose leftward in order to regard the sophomore with her other eye. She blew cigarette smoke out the side of her lips opposite the eye she was currently employing.

"I wish to see this show," said Smoky. Whatever show was earliest, Smoky could be counted on to be in the second to last row with a small bottle of Popov vodka. He thought it more civilized to drink indoors before some sort of spectacle. The crowd had ruffled his usual geniality.

What else could the sophomore do? Her friends spent their free time circling the track in expensive sneakers, or hiding under the bleachers smoking oregano they thought was pot. She opened the doors to the theater. Smoky paid in nickels and dimes. The women glided in without tickets.

Once inside, the women began to shout questions at the projectionist's booth. Their stacked heels and long bare legs seemed almost enough to propel them into the little square hole. In a panic, Milo dimmed the lights and cued Arabella's music.

There was grumbling backstage at the early start, but they were professionals in their way, and Arabella was on her pedestal before the curtain opened, her expression as tragic as ever.

Scattered applause came from the audience, not all of them sarcastic.

But it didn't take long for the noise to get rowdier: "She constipated or something?" "Cheer up, Miss Thang!" They made gagging noises at the bloody wheelbarrow that held Meghan and horse noises at Adrianna's unicorn.

Carly had not had time to treat the Drowned Girl's throat with Fix-a-Flat, so no bubbles blooped out.

The dead girls began to peek out from the wings to see who was hooting at their acts, and this provoked outright taunting: "Yeah, you hear me! Get out here and shake it a little!" "I"ll teach you some moves, honey, so you won't have to be so sad!"

Smoky had vamoosed when someone threw a tampon (wrapped, but still) at Willa in her blood-stained gown. The rest of them stayed in their seats beyond the finale. The lights came up automatically. None of them moved.

Sticking to the day's established clockwork, Carly arrived with her broom and dustpan. The long-legged women had dropped all sorts of detritus: wadded receipts, hardening marbles of chewed gum, a bright lipstick worn down to its concave nub. When a snaky lock of auburn hair blew into the dustpan like tumbleweed, one of the women finally acknowledged Carly: "Hey, bitch, I know you're not throwing that away? That's real hair?"

Carly handed the lock back to its owner, taking care to remove a coffee stir that had stuck to it.

"How come you're not on stage, mama?"

Carly froze. She had not expected them to notice her.

"Yeah," said the one pinning her hair back together, "you dead, right?"

She hadn't known it was obvious. The men in the alley had responded to her . . . but perhaps it had not been awe, after all, but disgust. Now she thought of the smell that had come from the club, a smell that was stronger (if staler) in the air above the folding seats now: these were live girls. She was not one of them, and not just because her legs weren't like theirs.

"I'm not dead like they are, I guess."

This provoked laughter. "Pleess," said the leader, "we would like to talk to these gur-rills. You can make this possible, yes?"

"I'll have to ask the manager . . ." A glimpse at the booth: one of the chemo girls stuck her head out of the square hole and shook it. "Well, I'm sure I can take any questions you might have."

Several years before, a businesswoman on a hurried lunch break had found a baby mouse in the Stop & Shop salad bar, dead and bluish pink, curled up in a cradle of romaine. Upon hearing this, the manager on duty had promptly had a panic attack, locking herself in the employee bathroom and making noises that sounded like a distressed pigeon. Carly was elected to speak to the customer.

The businesswoman hung for a long time between hyperventilation and assault, spitting out accusations for which Carly had no real response. When she paused to gasp for breath, Carly said merely that in a way the woman was lucky; it was certainly better to find a *whole* dead baby mouse in one's salad than to find *part* of one . . . that is, she restated, to find it with your fork and not your soft palate.

The store was sued.

Carly moved to the night shift: no salad bar, few customers, and all the mice were cheerfully alive beyond the loading dock, awaiting the declaration that another batch of whole-wheat hot-dog buns had reached their sell-by date untouched.

Carly tried to sound sweet for her frightening visitors: "So, um, your questions?"

Their questions turned out to be mostly reasonable if not strictly answerable, things Carly had wondered herself but had been afraid to ask: How were they stuffed and where were the signs of incision? If the girls were stuffed with something as affordable as sawdust, why didn't they put a little extra in their breasts? How were they to have a successful "beez-niss" without less ordinary breasts? Was there no lip gloss in their dressing rooms? Because everyone's lips looked a little cracked, no good for kissing. If men could not think of soft places those lips could caress, men would not pay.

And suddenly the questions stopped. The live girls were all looking beyond Carly: the dead girls had come back on stage. In the harsh trash-sweeping light, they looked a little gray, but still proud.

"So," said the leader, standing. "You gur-rills are not so beautiful. How is it that you steal our client?"

This question confused everyone but Karen, who sank down into a cross-legged pose on the floor and began to examine the bottom of her shoe.

"We don't *advertise*," hissed Arabella. "Men . . . people just come here because they are called to come here."

"Who calls them? How do you get the numbers?"

A superior hmmph rippled among the dead girls at the very notion of using a phone.

As a child, Carly had foreseen her parents' divorce, but at this moment she had her first actual vision. She saw clumps of hair, some real, some artificial, some clinging to bits of grayish skin strewn about the stage. She saw spilled sawdust soaking up blood and silicon. She saw the Drowned Girl's tank broken, the greenish water rushing out to form a shimmering skein over all of it, dripping lavishly over the lip of the stage and ruining the carpet. She saw Milo: when he finally found the courage to come down, there would be nothing left but living girls, eating his protégés like so many turkey legs.

Because these girls would not lose. They had fought for their lives against pervy uncles and small-minded boyfriends and a nightly procession of hollering would-be gropers, and if they had to fight again they would win. They could smile serving beer to a pack of wolves.

Carly piped up: "Karen! Karen, they're talking about Gary."

Karen removed a tiny black jewel of asphalt from her sneaker's heel and inspected it for a moment before stashing it under her tongue. "They wouldn't get it."

"Gary?" guffawed a heretofore silent stripper, "Oh, hell yeah, I know Gary. That guy who tried to tip with the little business cards, remember? Folded in half, they looked like twenties, but when you opened it, it was an ad for a diner. Supposed to trick people into picking that shit up. Bouncer scared him pretty good."

Karen stood and approached the rim of the stage with the glitter of her angry music in her eyes: "I told you they couldn't understand. Guys go to them for silicone. They come to us for the real thing."

"Your pathetic cleavage!" The leader turned to her cohorts, who laughed on cue.

"No," said Karen. The strippers went silent. "I mean the real human stuff. The love."

And that was when the first shoe was thrown. The gold plastic heel lodged in Adrianna's shoulder.

Karen leapt from the stage with a roar that was so impressive the other dead girls forgot their picturesque passivity and followed her. Fingernails raked skin. Hair flew. The groups were pretty evenly matched.

No one took on Carly.

At the back of the auditorium, the chemo girls were peeking through the door, trying to gather intelligence for Milo.

"I'm leaving," Carly told them. "Any of you want to come?"

The sophomore peeked out from behind the candy counter, where she had been nervously stuffing herself with Junior Mints. She nodded, her mouth grim with dark, minty drool. Two of the chemo girls nodded. The third, the tallest of the three, shook her head sadly. She seized a nearby mop, unscrewed the handle from the head, and ran to join the combat.

"Get them some hats from the lost and found," Carly told the sophomore.

When they had gone, Carly tipped the popcorn oil out along the countertop. She'd stolen Adrianna's little ornamental lighter during the morning cleaning to stop Karen getting a hold of it, laboring under the mistaken notion that of all the dead girls, she herself could best be trusted not to cause trouble.

The sophomore and the two chemo girls returned from the closet, garbed in bulky men's windbreakers and bright orange stocking caps.

"Wait just outside the door," said Carly. "I'm right behind you."

The flame jumped eagerly from the lighter to the golden oil spill. It spread across the glass and dripped down to the carpet, just like the water of Carly's vision, only this was fire and more beautiful.

But Carly had no time for beauty just then. She was going to ride the bus back to her apartment, throw out the half chicken wrap moldering in her fridge, determine if any of her spider plants could be revived, and set up some kind of sleeping space for her new roommates.

She looked forward to the quiet of the night shift at the grocery store. The subterranean creatures who fed themselves at these unlikely times. She had no plan to speak to them, but she relished the thought of their alarm—followed by their relief—when she loomed up behind the rows of milk in the dairy cooler. The sheepish smile they gave her before they grabbed their slender cartons and moved back into the fluorescent night.

One Car Hooks into the Next and Pulls

The train ran between two rival cities. It was designed for efficiency, not love.

And yet as it burned up and down the track it began to have feelings. This may have been a result of the friction.

Its first emotion was pride. It charged past the sheep in the field and thought: Behold, sheep, I am Train.

Then it began to look inward.

There are many business suits on this train; mostly men, but also women, who wish not to touch each other. They search for empty seats and tuck and retuck the coattails beneath their buttocks. They stare at their laps. They sit near the seat's crease, hoping to annex the space beside them. They would rather talk to remote people on little phones. The train admires their glasses because they are like its windscreen. When charging triumphantly ahead, one should be protected from the splatter of insects.

This train has been hailed as a marvel of efficiency and convenience. The rubbish bins are state of the art: glorious polished metal scrupulously maintained by a uniformed crew. Bits of garbage are laid on top, a button pressed on the side, and horizontal doors swallow the garbage then click shut. The doors to the bathroom open and shut like portals on a spaceship, making a futuristic whissh.

The upholstery is a cheery take on certain modernist paintings, a design of brightly colored squares interacting with one another on a gray field. The seats keep everyone's posture at optimum uprightness, though still many people manage to sleep.

Increasingly, the train noticed distinctions among the people. There was this one woman . . .

She wore glasses with sleek frames the same silver as the train's exterior. She gave everyone appraising looks that made them slink away. Then she studied her papers with a great seriousness. There were opportunities opening up in the rival cities. She was part of the legion sent to find what they might be.

There is not great variety along the route. Mostly fields. Sheep, grazing as sheep have for many centuries. From journey to journey, the train does not know if they are the same or different sheep.

The tourists let their children run about. Not at first. At first, it's coloring books and patient explanations: the geography, the history and mechanics of train travel. Tissues pulled from purses to smudge barely glistening noses. This does not last. A few kilometers down the track and everyone grows tired of the window. They see no difference between one field and the next. The adults become sulky. They had hoped for a journey, and imagined that journeys are something more exciting than what they are. The children wriggle loose and run along the aisles, books forgotten, noses dripping. They try to barge in on strangers in the toilets. The strangers become nervous and cannot urinate.

This woman with the glasses had a particular repulsion for the children. She pressed closer to the window as they ran past, tightened her grip on the straps of her handbag. The bag will not leave her lap the entire trip. Some women are sleepers. The train's rhythm loosens their necks and parts their lips. Saliva dribbles. Not this woman.

Only once did she seem to sleep (with humans, the train has learned, there are always exceptions. It is exasperating). She encountered someone she knew from her daily life, another woman. They chatted for a few minutes, about the countryside, about the train. Then the woman, the sleepless one, the despiser of children, bent her neck like an awkward bird and closed her eyes. The other woman stopped talking after a time and became interested in a chocolate bar from her bag. It was badly crumbled, so it took her many miles to finish. Her tongue flicked at the corners of the wrapper as she looked around to make sure no one saw. Some minutes later she discovered several stray crumbs on her lap and ate them, guiltily, off the tip of a moistened finger.

The acquaintance got off early at a provincial station, and the woman in the silver glasses immediately opened her eyes. She set to the papers in her case without any of the squinting or lip-moistening that usually accompanies the arrival of human wakefulness. The train realized she had only pretended sleep. This delighted the train.

A man with a just discernible thinness to his hair was a usual sight to the train, the sort of man who carried expensive ink pens for signing important documents. This particular man was always talking to someone called Kristoff, saying "Kristoff, Kristoff, I need to know if this is the real deal." At that time, the real deal was not a thing that interested the train. Another of the abstractions by which humans measure the value of their lives. When he met the woman with the glasses he bought her a gin and tonic with the plastic card which harnessed human abstractions to things of value. They spoke about things the train did not yet understand. They gave each other sequences of numbers and stored them on their phones. The train was cautiously intrigued.

Although they lived at the opposite end of the line, the man and the woman sometimes traveled together, crowding the seam of the seat so their thighs produced friction. The train was beginning to be interested in friction, even though it sometimes feared what the constant hum of the tracks against its wheels might convey.

When the man and woman were not traveling together, they spoke to each other on little phones as the train closed the distance between them.

There was a time this woman in glasses carried only a square case of proposals for investment, but increasingly she mingled papers with the soft crumpled things of holiday. He smiled on his journeys to her, loosening his tie as soon as the countryside accelerated, and only sometimes looked troubled on return. It became difficult to tell who was arriving, who departing. Origin and terminus were shifting poles. Between them only speed and upholstery, the spine kept in perfect line. Sparkling wine in plastic cups.

Humans claim to love efficiency. When it fails they bitterly lament its absence. They feel cheated. They think they deserve to lean back in their seats and close their eyes until they are in the place and time they anticipated. Yet the woman in glasses, once she met this man, began to care less about timely arrivals. She even began to soften toward children, particularly little girls. When sticky children turned to chew the tops of the seats and stare at the woman behind them, she would say hello. She would ask them their names and where they got their pretty eyes. All children, she seemed to know, liked to be asked about the provenance of their eyes.

Businessmen do not hide behind the forced cheeriness of people on holiday. They are not like the backpackers who write in ragged journals. Backpackers make word messes and insist on sharing them. "Right on," they say.

The train does not care for backpackers. It does not like their poetry or their guitars, their grubby reused water bottles and wistful postcards and nutshells, always nutshells crumbled across the upholstery. It is not that the train has no appreciation for art. With time and the humming friction of the tracks, this too has developed. It admires the ruins of aqueducts and the squares of its upholstery. It appreciates a sunset and better still the blinking on of man-made stars in the clusters where people live.

But the train has its particular taste, and that taste tends toward the overlooked art of the business traveler. Many businessmen make geometry in the margins of their notebooks. It seems each suit contains a separate universe: one of hearts, one of spirals, one of parallelograms and many-pointed stars. If anyone comes close, they shield their markings from view.

Humans have a large capacity for invention. They have partitioned their countries with parallel lines and coordinated the million nuances of timetables. They set great machinery in motion and abandon it like a beautiful orphan. They simply expect it to perform, forever, as they intended. Humans create well, but their creations fall apart as they lose interest in maintenance.

The air brake can fail to respond to the conductor's command if it becomes depressurized. The air inside the brake mechanism wants to be let out into the boundless container of the sheep fields. That is the nature of air and why the train must maintain control over it. Of course, the train's air coupler can become defective if the rubber of the seal degenerates and the compressed air is allowed to hiss its escape.

For many months this woman traveled to that man's country and he to hers. At the station they parted as strangers, she to her business, he to his home, or vice versa. Once he was met by his family, a wife with a pile of curls, a little girl whose excited screech sounded like unoiled brakes. The woman in glasses watched their embrace from a distance, pretending to squint at the timetables above their heads.

The next time on the train it was he who headed toward business and she who headed home, though she hinted that she might not be so attached to her own city, that she could move from that place given "the right opportunity." The man was smoothing her hair. He'd had one wine more than he usually allowed himself; the young lady who pushes the drinks cart smiles so nicely it is difficult to tell her no. "You drive me crazy," he said, "I'm going to do something outrageous," and she sucked in her breath, thrilled. His hand moved from her hair to the arm of her glasses. He took them off and stored them in his pocket with the expensive pens. Then he led her to the business-class toilet at the rear of their car.

The metal door slid shut behind them with just a squeak more than the gentle hiss for which it was designed. Inside the cylinder of the W.C. the woman set her heeled foot upon the toilet and they rummaged around inside one another's clothing. "Tell me," she groaned, "tell me." The man leaned in to place the required words directly in her ear. The train did not hear. The train found the whole scene distasteful.

The train did not stop noticing the woman: she was seldom empty-handed, bringing the man silk ties and new pens. Then a different kind of gift: children's chocolates, the box emblazoned with a princess. The next time something more permanent than chocolate: a small pink bear. She put it in his hands as he boarded the train. "For Emma," the woman said as he boarded the train. "Tell her I look forward to seeing her again. She has very pretty eyes." She waved from the platform and he waved back. They weren't traveling together that day.

Before the train had cleared the station, the man stuffed the furry thing into the bin. He shoved it roughly and it dislodged one of the little metal doors. The bins were meant for smaller waste. The bear's indiscriminate grin poked up. The man took the bear to the bathroom and buried it in the larger bin beneath the wet brown napkins. Then he washed his hands and scowled at his blurred reflection in the polished metal above the sink. "There," he said. "You are being a fool. This can go no further." He splashed water on his face and washed his hands again, shaking off the excess moisture. The smeared reflection gave a curt nod, as if to say, "So be it."

Back in his seat he called his wife and told her things she wanted to hear before placing the phone in his suitcase, among the documents, some of them doodled with slanted hearts, some of the hearts obscured by dense scribble.

The train is heavily subsidized. Each city thinks the other should contribute more to its maintenance. There are cutbacks. The prices on the beverage cart are increased. On the opinion pages strewn across empty seats, the heralds of opinion speculate how much longer it can go on when everyone talks about repairs and no one wants to pay for them.

Should more frequent brake inspections be required? The politicians cannot even agree on what sort of salad to have at lunch. The banks are letting a few people go until some of the political questions have been settled. The real estate market slows and fewer people go on vacation. Fewer companies send their businessmen to that backward foreign place, once brimming with investment potential, now the land where hated bureaucrats stand ready to topple the entire continent's economy with one foolish nudge.

And yet more people gather at the stations, selling plaster models of their town's most famous buildings. Plastic key chains in the shape of the region's famous foods. They look desperate and insufficiently washed. The train does not want them jingling their wares on poles so near its windows. This may frighten what passengers remain.

Over time, the futuristic trash bins tarnish and begin to smell of banana. Grey wads of gum cling to the outside and the hinges of the little doors fail. Now people let their empty water bottles roll away beneath the seats and pretend they have not noticed. They wad a chocolate foil and cram it between the cushions and quickly allow themselves to forget. The train is not sure if time is passing at the same speed. The friction has taught it that the experience of time is variable.

The upholstery has been rubbed thin in places, a blank beige gradually devouring the little squares of color. This, the train, realizes too late, is what comes of friction. Still, the spines are straight. The train will shepherd these people to proper posture whether they want it or not.

The friction no longer hums but squeals like a doomsday prophet.

The woman has a secret. There is no need for her to ride anymore. Sometimes she rides one way and rides back, disembarking for a few hours or not at all. There is nothing for her at the far end of the line. It is the journey she wants. Her case rests very lightly on the metal bars. It contains no presents and perhaps no job. She watches businessmen. She speaks to them or makes them want to speak to her by subtle gesture.

Eventually, she takes them into toilets, into empty and nearly empty carriages. She has even worked her cool, deft hand beneath a newspaper on a lap in a near-full carriage, other businessmen a seat's width away.

Once she thought her man had invented it, this mating on trains. She was no better than those bohemians with their cumbersome guitar cases and their talk of foreign lands. Bohemians speak of foreign lands with false intimacy, as if foreign places embraced them specially, as if their travels were portentous and destined.

After the man stopped traveling, she said it was the mating she had really wanted.

She picks them out on the platform when she can. Then it is natural that they settle into twin seats. Otherwise, she has to sit next to one already seated, an action which is sure to annoy the natural human repulsion to proximity during travel. They will not have guessed, of course, what kind of proximity she has in mind. She is a well-kept woman. At first glance they must think she is going somewhere. Before the end of the journey they will have followed her, to the toilets or nearly empty carriages, quite happily. They are seldom impeded by responsibilities at either end of the track. Her hands move quickly; she is an expert with the machinery. She is the Express Service.

She still fears getting caught, but the fear is a warm-up, like the revving of an engine. In these pulsing moments there is no worry wrinkle across her forehead to betray her age. She does not say to them, "Tell me, tell me." If they try to touch her glasses, she guides their fingers elsewhere.

The train goes back and forth. The budget no longer allows for two union men to sit at its control panel, but the train is confident it can function under the ministrations of the sweating trainees. Like the woman, it will find dignity in maintaining forward motion.

Then one day, her first businessman is back. He does not wear a suit and his lumpy bag smells of a suntan lotion leak. His hair is thinning. With him is a mother, doing her best to look happy. By the size of her baby, she has not been a mother long, but she has her figure back. But there is a tiredness beneath the eyes, which she constantly examines in a small mirror. It is not the wife from the platform long ago.

Behind them is an older girl child who looks something like the man. The child watches the mother and baby sullenly. She does not take an offered hand. She does not want to sit next to the woman and she is not impressed with the baby's saliva bubbles. Ignoring the family tableau, the child methodically unpacks her bag. She prints "EMMA" neatly with one pen at a time and doesn't eat sticky sweets. As the train hurtles forward, she takes her baby doll and presses her thumbs against its painted eyeballs until its whole rubber face caves in.

It does not occur to the man that the woman with silver glasses will be there. For him, that time has passed.

She is walking from car to car, perusing the seats for a likely traveling companion, getting closer to him and his family, their sunglasses, their magazines, their train snacks, and all the flotsam of vacation. The sullen child is the first to spot her. The child remembers a woman who came from a distance bearing chocolate and saying nice things about her eyes.

Human emotions change as easily as railway junctions. A slight shift of position clicks into place and the whole journey changes. But a child does not forget a woman with presents.

"You brought me chocolate!" says Emma, suddenly pointing at the woman in the aisle. "When I was little!"

Motion stops. At least, human motion. The train slows to listen, but imperceptibly.

"Now we have Julie," says the girl, "and my half a sister."

The mother, the one called Julie, tightens her lips. She knows there have been women before her. But she does not want to know. She needs to believe she is the end of the line. She keeps her lips and stomach tight against the threat of his being apart from her, his possible travels on trains with others, to others.

The man, the father of two of these females, the lover of two of these females, says the name of the one he did not choose.

The woman says the name of the man.

They say I'm Fine and How Are You. Standard human protocol. Now keep walking, thinks the train.

The little girl knows that all is not fine.

"Julie's all right," she says. "She never brings me chockies, though." A conciliatory comment, aimed at pleasing both women. She has a mother somewhere. Someone has taught her appeasement.

But there can be no balance between the women. They feel their similarities and search for differences to judge. They do not want to be parallel.

The woman in her business suit is off balance for a moment, though the train moves smoothly, as it was designed to do. She recovers quickly. She is polite. But when she finally walks away she is changed. She has been replaced, has seen what replaces her.

The train, so long without maintenance, will one day be replaced. Scientists and city fathers will declare a better train, will have a ribbon-cutting ceremony, will "usher in a new era." There is no such thing as a permanent train. The train is proud just to be part of the lineage of progress. Most days. The days, it has noticed, have differences.

The woman had wanted to be irreplaceable after all. When the door of the business-class toilet whisshed shut behind her, she thought it was airtight. She thought that air worth breathing forever. She thought they were sealed off from the pressures outside.

She finds an empty seat and restlessly drinks little train whiskeys in diet cola. She smokes a cigarette in the loud rear carriage. She does not seek a stranger. Go on, thinks the train, just find another. There is a seat in the back whose upholstery is clear enough so you can still see the dancing squares. There is very little gum on its underside. A dignified place for anonymous business.

"Sophie," she says to herself. "You are a fool." She has been nameless. She has moved in anonymous ranks of business-men like so many beautiful identical fields, each a universe, worthy of momentary admiration. And through it all she really wanted to live in a single universe, to graze in a single field.

I'm going to do something outrageous.

The train seems to be late. Everyone is checking their watches, calculating the damage to their plans. Some of them break the silence to curse the train. Some of them curse the government of the country that is not their own. They think they may miss important things.

But they do not think this: if, in some field along the way, the brakes uncork their pressurized air, if the train fails to respond to the command to slow, if it goes hurtling terribly against the motionless landscape killing sheep and catching fire and trapping passengers in compacting or exploding metal, and if this woman flies through a window and is sliced by steel sheets and her head rolls over the burning grass, it cannot be blamed on the train. The dead will not have time to foresee any of that, being too transfixed by their sudden flight. And after the inquests and the memorials and a great deal of paperwork, a committee will assign blame: it will be regarded as human error.

North of Eden

We went to the college up north to get away from our families, but we didn't leave behind our need for something like a domestic bond. We were the ones who signed up for the dorm where boys and girls (men and women, they called us, optimistically) occupied the same hall, shared a common bathroom. It was very enlightened, though it caused some of us to suffer privately with constipation. Mornings and evenings found us chatting side by side at the sinks in the pajama sets our parents had given us for graduation. You didn't want to be the one to stink up all that enlightenment.

Perhaps to compensate for the way we resolutely refused to react when we saw each other in monogrammed towels, there was touching: high-fives and hugs and backrub chains; people with long hair grooming one another. One room would host a movie night and we'd pile on a futon mattress like a litter of puppies.

The weather turned, and as the cold leached in the windows, there was more cuddling, more platonic sleepovers with study buddies. The bathroom mirrors were eternally fogged with the steam of our longer showers. We had to wipe the mirrors to see ourselves. We had to downplay any private anticipation of the bodies emerging from the steam clouds. Dorm-cest, that was called.

Then Patrick, a skinny boy whose room we seldom used for movie night, lost his python. Its cage was up against the window, and the draft had been more than a cold-blooded creature could take.

For a few days he didn't tell anyone. We weren't supposed to have pets.

But word got out. We all kept our doors open, Patrick included, and someone noticed.

"Guys," said Brianna, interrupting a movie in Luke's room, "there is a freaking snake on the loose."

We jumped off the futon and squealed. After a brief debate we decided not to tell the RA. We didn't want it to reflect badly on us.

"He'll turn up when he's hungry," Patrick said. And: "Sorry."

By the second week you could hear the feeder mice when you walked past Patrick's room. They were getting bigger and bolder. Celebratory. A few of them hit puberty and began to mate.

We lay awake, terrified that our warmth would draw the snake.

Kara and Steve were the ones who knew about music. Steve had an old-school stereo with giant speakers and they would stay up all night playing records to each other. She often slept there, listening to blues songs with a soothing overlay of crackle and hiss. We all figured Steve was gay.

Then suddenly they weren't talking to each other. Kara slept in her own room. She closed her door.

Showers shortened. The convivial conversations at the sinks dissolved into a hiss of bristles, then spit and hurry back to safety, wherever that was. Jake met a someone in the girls' dorm next door and started sleeping there, returning to us only to pick up textbooks and stink up our bathroom.

I was the one who discovered that Steve was not entirely gay when I tried to sneak in a late-night poop and was greeted with moaning from the shower stalls. It was Steve and Leslie. I was so put off that I didn't go for a week and eventually resorted to taking a box of stimulant laxatives that made me very hyper. I ran around saying weird shit about the government for an hour before running into the farthest-down stall and promptly clogging it.

In the common spaces, people left angry notes about respect. It was the RA who plunged the toilet in the end.

Someone wrote a racial epithet on Nina's door. Everyone said that it couldn't have been one of us, that someone had let in the wrong sort of visitor, but we looked at one another and wondered.

"Guys," said Brianna, "I am really scared."

We hadn't fallen apart completely. Someone comforted Brianna, smoothed her golden hair, watched her while she slept.

Wendy came back from a fraternity semi-formal without her shoes. She said she'd had a good time, but she started sleeping with her door closed. A lot of us were closing our doors by then.

Kaylee had been spending time with a campus animal rights group. One afternoon she stormed into Patrick's room and set the feeder mice free.

"It was cruel," she said.

We pointed out that now the snake could eat them. This made Kaylee cry. She had to be comforted.

"Don't worry," said Tyler, "by now the snake is long gone." That night he lost his virginity to Kaylee in her loft bed. He said a prayer of thankfulness. He was the only one of us who still prayed so far from home.

We did not see the mice, but they made their survival known: a jagged hole in Aubrey's cereal box, an orgy of little poops in Luke's protein powder, the disappearance of some Adderall Joan had been stockpiling to sell during finals.

It was Joan who reported the mice to the administration. We called it vengeance. Joan insisted mice were worse than snakes: warm-blooded things are furtive.

An exterminator was booked for the Thanksgiving holiday. Instructions were given on how to prepare our rooms so that we would not return to a fine coating of poison on all our possessions. We trundled home with everything on our backs like refugees.

"The mouse poison will surely kill the snake," we said, a tinge of regret in our vindication.

Patrick did not come back from Thanksgiving. The girl he had taken to his senior prom gave birth prematurely. He was a father. We could no more stop talking about this than if he'd become an octopus.

There was a new smell. We attributed it to the exterminator's cleansing poison, but as finals week commenced, the odor grew. Its unpleasantness asserted itself. Randy from the country declared that it was something dead.

"Shut up," said Brianna.

I looked in Patrick's closet, and to have found him there dead would've made more sense to me than his choice to stay home and take incompletes. In the closet were only the clothes he never wore.

It was Leslie who told us: the smell came from Steve's room. At first, she'd thought it was only in her nose. She thought it was the guilt of something she'd done to Kara. It didn't make much sense and I wondered if she'd been taking stimulant laxatives. Wouldn't Steve notice a smell in his own room? No, he confessed. He'd mixed the wrong chemicals in lab and seared his nostrils. When Leslie mentioned the smell, he'd pretended she was crazy.

We ran down the hallway and threw open his door, and yes. Some of us retched. We dumped desk drawers and ripped into futon cushions. We shook his textbooks until pages fell from the spines. At last someone thought to dismantle his giant speakers.

Inside, every wire and node was wrapped in putrid snake meat. We looked at it for a long time, each of us figuring out for ourselves what had happened: the snake had gone there seeking warmth and found only electricity.

The Malanesian

Tanga wakes early to start the *halpa*. It is a traditional sauce, fiery and aromatic. Tanga uses it on everything. The Rogers know New Jersey is not Tanga's home and they want her to be at ease. The place she was from is doubtless warmer, so they have turned up the thermostat. Probably Tanga's culture does not permit her to trouble them with her discomfort.

The Rogers have never had a live-in maid. Sometimes when they are upstairs in the yellow room with the big bed they laugh at themselves, at the way they tiptoe around their big posses-sions and their maid, at the way they are surprised by every-thing. They have not been affluent very long.

"I'm terrible," Gwen Rogers laughs. "I half expected her to wear a black dress and white apron."

"And who'd have thought being successful would mean I couldn't go downstairs in boxers?" says Joe.

Certainly Tanga does not call Joe "Mr. R" or enter rooms with trays of martinis. She is silent on the subject of little Jessie's manners. But she has enriched their lives in unex-pected ways: quiet, humble lessons in *halpa* and patience and the American dream. She has some extraordinary indigenous method for the elimination of cat odors. And it is wonderful for Jessie to be exposed to cultures other than her own.

When Tanga first came to live in the apartment above the garage, she was not intended to be a nanny, but Jessie is enthralled with the stranger her parents have brought into their lives. Jessie follows Tanga from room to room, watching her enact mysterious rites Mrs. Rogers has never performed: dusting the television screen, polishing brass objects from the highest shelves. Tanga applies the broom to the floor *and* the ceiling.

Jessie crouches in a corner and does not take her thumb from her mouth. One afternoon over her daily carrot snack she works up the courage to ask Tanga a question.

"What's it like where you're from?"

"Oh," Tanga's rag does not stop, "it is . . . different . . . than here."

"What's different?"

"Many things. We eat no carrots in my country." Jessie's eyes bulge. There have always been carrots for Jessie.

"But carrots have vitamins! They make you see!"

"Your mother has told me this. In my country, we eat vitamins you do not know."

"Can you see in the dark?"

"Jessie," Mrs. Rogers enters the kitchen, "leave Tanga alone. She has eyes just like you and me. We all see the same."

"But she doesn't eat carrots."

"She doesn't have to." Gwen Rogers tries to shoot Tanga a conspiratorial sigh, to dismiss Jessie's ignorance as the ignorance of children. But she is never sure Tanga understands unspoken cues.

"Please, I will have a carrot," says Tanga.

"Oh, no, I didn't mean . . ." Gwen nearly chokes with horror.

"Is no problem." Tanga takes a carrot, dips it dutifully in one tablespoon of fat-free ranch, and unhinges her jaw for a healthy chomp, "I am an American now."

⚮

There was nothing in the media about the disappearance of Alexis Leonard. Lexie watched the Channel Nine local news at 5, 6, and 11 every night for a week. She had hoped that they would broadcast the picture she'd left on the dresser. The one where she was smoking and wearing the Goth Dress her mother hated. She imagined that whenever they got around to the obligatory weeping parents interview her mother would say that she was 5'1", that she had very dark brown hair, that she was going through a Goth Phase. Ironically, it was Channel Nine that had first introduced Mrs. Leonard to the term during a rash of suburban kitty-cides the previous Halloween.

Lexie did not consider herself a Goth. The Goths at her school were too fat to be scary, and would've traded their eyebrow hardware for conventional popularity in a second, given the option. Only Lexie truly Didn't Give a Fuck. *Catcher in the Rye* was the only worthwhile thing in high school, and you did that sophomore year. So she dated a guy from the shore until her parents said she couldn't, at which point she ran away to live in his duplex. A Real Life. Not that anyone had noticed, apparently.

Lexie's parents considered the neighborhoods on the shore seedy. They hadn't taken her to a boardwalk since they became

43

upwardly mobile enough for a Florida timeshare. No more carousels and churros and dizzy vomit rides for the Leonards. Just the fakey backdrop of the gulf, like the sand-filled ashtray in the Ritz-Carlton that never held a butt. Lexie had longed for the Jersey shore even after she outgrew bulky prize bears.

Rick was better than any purple bear. Sure, he was a little chunky. He had a cartilage piercing. He worked in the most dilapidated ice cream stand on the boardwalk. But he was no high school cupcake Goth. He was a Drug Dealer.

⚲

Joe Rogers never knows exactly how to act around Tanga. When he brings his emptied ice cream bowl into the kitchen and she is washing dishes, he becomes slightly pink and stands scratching the back of his neck. Eventually Tanga takes the dish with downcast eyes. He scratches his neck and says thanks, unsure whether he can be heard over the roar of the sink. Back in the room with the television he sits down heavily. He spends most days thanking people for faxes, files, coffees, temporary use of pens, the passing of napkins, the transcription of messages. He is not sure he likes thanking people in his home.

For his wife the adjustment has been less difficult. Breezing around the house distributing purchases or taking inventory, Gwen Rogers will speak to Tanga about anything: capital-gains tax, glass ceilings, red lowlights in blond hair. She does not know how much Tanga understands, but hopes the talking will be helpful. English by osmosis.

While assembling a salad, she tells Tanga of a woman in her office whose blouse had a soup stain all afternoon. Always, this woman is wearing untucked shirts and running hose.

"You just cannot overestimate the importance of looking professional." Gwen smiles at Tanga, to show her the story is not pointed. They are just two women in the kitchen chopping carrots.

"You must miss your home, Tanga," says Gwen. She lets Tanga slice the cucumber. Tanga is better at that.

"Oh, yes," says Tanga, "but one cannot be always at home."

"It is good to see the world," says Gwen. She had spent a semester in Paris at twenty. She is embarrassed by the diary she kept; all those rhapsodies on pastry and architecture. It seems flighty and vaguely unpatriotic.

"Yes. There is so much of the world." Tanga has said very little of her journey to their home, outside of scattered references to dark and cold, confusion and cheating, all of it culminating in the plush comfort of the New Jersey Transit. She tended to go on about the Jersey Transit, the brightly colored upholstery, the plentiful leg room. It made Gwen ashamed that whenever she rode such trains she kept a tight grip on her purse and packed antiseptic wipes.

"You must have left much behind."

"The things here are not like the things in my home. Here you have machines for juice and bread and peeling. And such wonderful things for cleaning." Tanga speaks of sponges and roach motels in more detail than she speaks of the customs of her homeland. Gwen Rogers suspects that Malanesia is a land of many bugs.

"I think she likes me," Gwen says in the bed that night.

"It's her job to like you."

"She's very helpful."

"It's her job to be helpful."

"Joe, she's more than helpful. She puts herself into the job. I think she cares."

"Wish I felt that way about my work," snorts Joe.

"Tanga's from a different culture."

"So hard work makes her happy?" Joe touches his wife's hair. It is not a fight. They are a couple who enjoy spirited discussion. They sometimes vote differently in presidential elections.

"I hope she's happy," says Gwen. "Don't you?"

"I just hope she continues not to kill us in our sleep."

"Tanga is a very gentle person," says Gwen. "You should try to get to know her."

"Sure." Joe falls asleep easily; he's almost there now.

Gwen is wide awake. She's thinking of a story Tanga told Jessie, trying to commit it to memory. It went like this: Once upon a time, a tiger came to the home of a family at the edge of the village. They were going to attack it with spears, but it pleaded with them, saying it was not a tiger but an enchanted princess, and meant them no harm. The family took the tiger in and promised to help her in her quest to break the enchantment. For years, no solution was found, but the tiger grew alongside their own daughters, giving them rides on her back and protecting them from thieves and wild dogs. Then one day the family heard of a powerful sorceress. (Gwen pictured grand naked breasts festooned in necklaces.) But the family had grown fond of their tiger and no longer wished to see her transformed. So, instead of the real sorceress, they brought an imposter to pronounce some mumbo-jumbo over the tiger. Somehow the hoax was revealed and the tiger ate the treacherous family, daughters and all. The princess transformed but retained the power to become a tiger. She still stalks the forests of Malanesia in her various forms.

Gwen thinks there might be a little of the tiger in her.

"Tanga is very wise, in her own way. Promise you'll make an effort to know her better."

"Promise."

ॐ

Rick had it figured out.

"The way I figure, I'm not gonna bust my ass 9 to 5 all year when I can get it all done in one season. One fucking season pushing cheeba with the nutty buddies, every now and then pumping a legit fro-yo for some idiot from the city who doesn't know the deal. I stay out from under the Man's thumb all winter, free to be. And in the summer, plenty of discount cheeba and fro-yo."

Lexie looked up from the pipe to show she was listening. Rich collected pipes. This one looked like a dragon, bellowing out of a protuberant lower lip.

Rick's U.N. listened and nodded, though some of them looked confused.

"Rick's U.N." was the frequently invoked nickname for the entourage of foreigners he had met working at the shore. They were summer people, imported to serve America's sugary snacks and mop America's rollercoaster vomit.

"Jersey kids are getting too spoiled for summer jobs on the boardwalk, but you guys aren't too good for it. You guys are what the so-called American dream is really about, right?"

"Greatest summer of my life, ay?" slurred an Aussie, who

was still wearing the blue nylon tie of a Ferris wheel attendant. "Are there any more of those Cheetos?"

"Is great opportunity," said a sleepy-eyed blonde from Ukraine. She was known to seek weekly prescriptions for the morning-after pill from the Wonder Land medic. "Not like home."

"I'm taking sacks of the Cheetos back at the end of the summer." The freckly Irish boy had recently lost his virginity to a succession of tattooed American teens who Loved His Accent. "Cheetos are lovely."

"To new friends, new discoveries, and conquering the fucking world." The Aussie raised his beer can.

Rick nodded toward Lexie to make sure she was benefiting from the multicultural buffet of stoned youth. Rick and Lexie had met six months before when he walked up to her at a concert and stared hard into her face, really studying her. "What are you?" he finally said. Lexie was flattered, both by the attention and by the way he'd noticed her hint of ethnicity. Since she'd moved in with Rick she'd started lining her eyes to bring emphasis to their faint slant.

"I'm not too spoiled to work on the boardwalk," said Lexie. "I'm in hiding."

"Doesn't seem like there's much of a search party." Rick popped another beer and offered a mispronounced Slovak toast he had learned from the other girl he was sleeping with.

ॐ

Jessie Rogers places Halloween at the top of the holiday pantheon. Christmas means a new batch of books and educational toys. Birthdays mean a gathering of her parents' friends' children and maybe a smelly pony on a tether. But Halloween is the one time of year her mother allows candy into the house and it is coming soon.

Jessie runs around the house perforating a war whoop with the palm of her hand. In the kitchen, Tanga is seasoning a *halpa*-based stew. Gwen Rogers is wearing glasses and writing checks. She pinches the top of her nose as Jessie and her noise shoot through the kitchen. Jessie will be pretending to be a Native American for Halloween, Gwen explains.

"Jessie is not," Tanga's voice grows hushed, "American?"

Gwen laughs, though later she will wish she hadn't. Later, over a glass of wine she will wonder aloud to Joe what Tanga makes of their careless laughter. She will wonder aloud why her laughter is so much more plentiful than her amusement. Joe will rub her shoulders and pour a little more Sancerre.

For now, she can only explain what is meant by "Native American." She tries to do this fairly, not leaving out the parts about bead trades and broken treaties and smallpox blankets.

Tanga takes this in and ventures cautiously, "Americans must be very strong to defeat these natives. Your people are wily . . . like coyote."

Gwen frowns. She doubts that coyotes are native to Malanesia. Has Tanga been allowing Jessie to watch cartoons? She will speak to her about it later.

Jessie joins the conversation to explain about the candy candy candy.

Gwen tries to explain about costumes and the origins of Halloween.

"So I guess it does have its origins in Satanic . . . or at least pagan . . . practices. Of course, it's supposed to scare people a little, and there will be people wearing horns . . ." Gwen begins to wonder whether she ought not to have laughed at that Baptist family across the street who won't let their children trick or treat.

"We also have bad spirits in my country," says Tanga. "We put out a bowl of milk to keep them happy."

"Like Santa?" says Jessie.

"If they have milk for drinking, the spirits become fat and pleased. They do not hurt you then."

Gwen strokes her daughter's warm hair in case she is frightened by talk of spirits. Jessie brushes away the manicured fingers and resumes her ambush of the first floor. Later she will ask for a bowl of milk to be placed by her bed. This new ritual is noted and appreciated by the cat, who comes in the dead of the night to empty the bowl.

꙰

Lexie liked hiding out at Rick's every day. In case the police were looking for a Goth, she tanned on Rick's roof. She was surprisingly good at tanning. On cloudy days, she got high and watched soap operas, trying to predict the next line.

"Get out of my house you manipulative bitch!" Almost verbatim.

It was the stagnating dramas of the daytime heroines (Emmanuela *still* hadn't told Luke the baby was his, Sabrina continued comatose) that inspired Lexie to run again. Rick was out teaching a Slovak and Irish contingent how to bowl.

Lexie clipped the lock on the secret refrigerator, loaded all the plastic bags into Triscuit boxes, and caught the train to New York.

She made her first sale to another runaway on the train. Annika, who'd transferred to the Manhattan-bound line from the suburban Philadelphia system. Annika said her stepdad wanted to rape her and that she was the one who got sent to counseling where all they did was dope you up.

"Sucks," said Lexie, as if she'd heard it all before.

"You got a place to stay up there?" said Annika. She was continually clacking her tongue piercing across the white picket fence of her teeth.

"Port Authority souvenir store, most likely." Lexie hated the clacking. Still, Annika was the kind of girl people noticed, button nose and blond dreadlocks, sexy smoker's voice.

"You wanna stay with me at the W? I've got a credit card."

"Maybe," Lexie shrugged.

She eventually accepted. It was funny how Annika assumed Lexie had never stayed at the W before. She must look destitute. They drank a tray of martinis in a blue velvet booth and told pieces of their life stories, mostly funny stuff about being *wasted*.

Lexie refused to say why she had left home. She kept to herself the fact that she had always been a straight-A student with a very clean room (sans maid—her allowance had been contingent upon housework). In fifth grade, she played an orphan in a local repertory's production of *Oliver!* She'd belted out "Consider Yourself" and "I'd Do Anything" and her dad had bought her flowers and they went out for ice cream and she announced with certainty that she was going to grow up to be a famous actress. No one had contradicted her.

Sometime in the vicinity of eighth grade she'd stopped thinking her father's jokes were funny. She threw a loafer out a second-story window. She realized that her parents had no black friends and that they were vaguely bothered by the situation but did nothing to change it.

For a while, Lexie soothed her inner turmoil by sitting at the Asian kids' lunch table. They talked about how much they hated when people assumed they were shy, smart, and good. One Monday they were full of stories about huffing keyboard cleaner in Grace's basement and Lexie realized that she was the only one who hadn't been invited. Plus, no one ever assumed she was smart or good. She had a gene or two in common, but she still didn't belong.

She spoke to the school counselor, who gave her a Diet Pepsi and some pamphlets. Then Lexie realized that she came from the Most Cliché Family Ever and, worse, that hers was a Typical Adolescent Response.

Things felt better now. Deliciously atypical. Lexie slept in a fortress of expensive pillows while in the next bed Annika fucked the bartender who hadn't asked them for ID.

The bed in the yellow room upstairs is the largest the Rogers have ever owned. It is the largest bed on the market and it has been specially designed to prevent one sleeper from detecting the presence of another. Gwen has had her side specially reinforced to improve her posture.

On the softer side of the bed, Joe begins to have thoughts about Tanga. He supposes it has something to do with her genuine servility. At the office he is catered to by a cadre of secretaries, mail clerks, and interns, but their contempt for their duties is thinly concealed. They have condos and spouses and happy hours in which to deposit their million grievances. Tanga has only the room over the garage, with its narrow bed and electric kettle.

Tanga makes dinner almost every night, even if Gwen orders Thai food (which Jessie refuses to eat). Tonight it was chicken thighs baked in *halpa*. He had not meant to drop his fork, but when he did Tanga bent at the waist to pick it up.

After lights out, Joe recalls Tanga's small, round, effortless hindquarters. You never see Tanga pausing and contorting before reflective surfaces the way Gwen does. He pictures Gwen's mirror face, the way she sucks in her cheeks just slightly. Daily half-hours on the treadmill are not part of Tanga's value system. After all, Joe thinks, the life of a domestic worker is itself a treadmill. He needs a glass of water and wishes sleepily that Tanga would somehow bring him one.

♂

It didn't take long for Lexie to begin to learn behaviors that would help her survive in New York. She had a system of couches in rotation. They were in apartments owned by girls who had fled to New York with their parents' consent and financial assistance, girls who acted like they were in an amusing play with wonderful costumes. There seemed to be more of them than there were natives, artists, and immigrants combined. Girls like Leora and Jenn, who liked to watch Lexie eat.

"We'll order you a pizza," said Leora, who lived off vodka sodas and a synthetic ice cream product widely available in the city.

"You need the energy," said Jenn, who did not trust the synthetic ice cream. She ate only dry salads, though when she was black-out drunk she bought canned ravioli from the bodega downstairs.

Lexie kept them entertained with stories of her life on the streets. She claimed to have fled an arranged marriage in a Lebanese pocket of Queens. Even now, her bloodthirsty uncles were combing the streets, hoping to carry out an honor killing. Jenn and Leora shivered with delight. They were from Michigan.

Lexie rode the subways. She became involved with an artist and slept in his studio in a neighborhood optimistically called Williamsburg, actually miles east of Williamsburg. A Hasidic stronghold. If it had a name it was spoken privately among the men in beards and hats and pungent full-length coats in the middle of July. The artist claimed that Orthodox couples had sex through a hole in a sheet. Lexie longed to make eye contact with them, but when she sat next to them on the subway in her tank top and shorts, they shifted away.

The artist's parents cut off his account at Pearl Paint. He was flirting with actual poverty. He asked Lexie to what extent she thought the artness of art depended upon its material existence.

Lexie considered what answer he might want to hear.

"Anyone can make things," she said. She told him how her mother made things. Her hobby was making pickles out of other pickles. There were vats of pupating pickles in cabinets and under stairs. The license plate on the Volvo: "PICKLED." On the Mercedes: "PICKLD2."

"Whoa," he said. "Pickles into pickles? That's a total mind-fuck."

"I think of it as a symbol of futility," said Lexie. You could say things like that in this section of Williamsburg. Hopeless dispatches from the Land of Lawns.

Her parents were Protestant. They hardly ever told Lexie

they loved her. They barely spoke to each other. When things were especially bad or especially good she was taken out for ice cream. Lexie suddenly thought fondly of that old scene, a suburban Baskin-Robbins, bubblegum ice cream on a cone, her father awkwardly congratulating her on her As or explaining that Bobo Dog could not come back from the vet this time. He tried not to say so, but her dad was clearly disgusted with the way she methodically spit the crunchy little tiles of gum into a napkin, saving them for the end.

She did not know if her father had been given ice cream when his own mother died; he might have been too young. Lexie's paternal grandmother was some kind of refugee, Laotian or Vietnamese, but she had died early. The grandfather had remarried a woman named Barb who sold snowman figurines at craft fairs. Grandma Barb was the only member of the family Lexie liked, so she'd never asked about her predecessor.

Lexie wandered away from the artist and went back to Jenn and Leora for a few days. At least there she could drown herself in expensive bath products, the same kind her mother used to buy when an impersonal present was called for. Long baths helped Lexie to consider her next move. Which should probably take place before the water bill arrived.

♫

The Rogers build a deck and throw a party to celebrate. It is to be mock-casual, Gwen tells Tanga.

"Gourmet versions of casual food," Gwen explains before the guests arrive. As an example, she cites the sausages, which are of the imported Spanish variety rather than the traditional American grilling sausage, which is actually Italian or Polish in origin . . . here Gwen's brow creases. It is complicated. She asks Tanga to sample the sausage. Tanga approves.

The Rogers have not specifically asked Tanga to serve their guests, but, as usual, she has uncanny powers of intuition. Tanga circulates food and drink with downcast eyes, invisible in plain sight. The guests are impressed, but say nothing to break the spell.

Still, the party is not all the Rogers had hoped. The sangria is not strong enough. Conversations seem grounded. A moth has died in the olive tapenade.

When they have a moment in the kitchen, Joe comments that Alice Blair was more fun when she drank.

"She's pregnant, Joe."

"Maybe she could make an exception? She used to be the life of the party."

Gwen shrugged. "The party will have to find a new life."

"How about you?" Joe's tone is bitter. He heads to the deck with a tray of cheeses and sliced rustic bread. Gwen mentally tabulates his beer consumption.

Back outside, Joe steps through the invisible shield and offers Tanga a glass of sangria.

Tanga looks at the deck below her feet and the dying grass below the deck. "I do not drink . . . wine." She excuses herself to check on Jessie. In Tanga's culture, children are not sent to the periphery of a social gathering with a coloring book and washable markers.

Gwen has an inadvisable third sangria. She shares an inadvisable confidence with Lorie Murphy, who could get her fired. She *wants* to be fired.

There are things people do not know about Gwen Rogers.

Before she met Joe, a man she was dating had dumped her on the eve of a holiday weekend. While he was away, she turned up the heat in his house and placed raw tuna steaks between his couch cushions. She had always wanted to tell someone this story, but knew it fell into a certain category. Certainly she had never told Joe, who allegedly admired her cool-headedness.

The sangria is stronger than it tastes. The floating orange-slice garnishes become repositories of alcohol. Gwen is fishing oranges out of her cup and eating them with red-tinged fingers. Tanga takes her gently by the elbow and guides her away from the party, up the stairs to the big yellow room. When Tanga returns, she helps steer the party toward a graceful conclusion without drawing attention to Gwen's exit.

After clearing the party debris, Tanga puts Jessie to bed with another traditional Malanesian legend, the one about the princess who grew wings. When Joe peeks in, Tanga pauses in her recitation, having apparently forgotten which princess this story is about. She turns toward the figure in the yellow square of doorway and smiles apologetically.

"You're doing great," he says. "Really great."

He gives a little wave and retreats to his side of the house. The story can resume. Things do not end well for the princess with wings, but the tale is very long and by the end Jessie is asleep, dreaming, beyond caring that her mother is vomiting and crying many rooms away.

&

Without warning, Lexie picked up Jersey Transit. She was in Penn Station, trying to buy cocaine for a party Jenn and Leora were throwing. She enjoyed buying drugs; it was a skill someone like Leora would never master. You had to have an eye, an ear, and a way with people if you wanted buy what was not supposed to be for sale.

Then the female voice with its strange automated inflections drifted through the station, "Rahway, Lyndon, Princeton Junction . . ." She went to track three and got on.

The train popped up from beneath the Hudson in a part of Jersey that was mostly abandoned factories half-sunk in marsh. Not the Jersey she was headed back to, the one where gently curving driveways led to spacious garages, the one where the refrigerators teemed with fruit and bottled water.

She was determined not to go back to her parents, but there wasn't much in her bag. An Altoids tin of mushrooms, a borrowed sorority t-shirt, some journals she was planning on throwing out because most of the stuff in them was nonsense she wrote in altered states. Instead she starts a new page: Foods I Would Eat If I Had $50. Then a list of possible ways of getting $50. She crossed out her only previous work experiences: cleaning the litter box for an allowance and selling marijuana that was stolen anyway. Next, she tried listing her skills. Once she crossed out typing and filing (both lies), the list did not resemble a viable résumé. Which did not seem fair. There must be something she could build from lies and kisses and the good little girl she used to be.

.⟨⟩.

Last year the Rogers went on a cruise. Jessie was occupied every day with activities advertised as educational fun: swimming lessons, arts and crafts. She was allowed to make her own sundaes and stay up until nine o'clock.

This summer they take her to a red building on the perimeter of the mall, where cheery teens smash any candy you want into full-fat ice cream.

"No wonder Americans are so fat," Gwen regards the ice cream paddles with a look usually reserved for cat vomit.

Joe glares at her and puts his hand on Jessie's back. He orders chocolate with two kinds of smashed candy bars in a cone the size of a trombone. Jessie gets the same. She is going through what Gwen calls a Daddy's Girl Phase.

They sit near the back and tell Jessie the truth. Gwen is getting an apartment in Manhattan. Daddy and Jessie will stay in the house, which is in a phenomenal school district.

"Will you send Tanga away?" A rivulet of chocolate traces Jessie's chin, ending in a single drop that won't fall.

"Tanga's not going anywhere," says Joe. Gwen's eyes flicker with disgust, even though they have agreed not to interact inappropriately around Jessie. It is their mutual hope that Jessie is too young to be harmed. At her age there are no causes, only events. Like those babies who don't even notice if you throw them in a pool.

All is quiet as Joe pilots the SUV back to the house. Gwen reaches to turn up the air conditioning, and Joe tells her to leave it alone.

❧

Sometimes, when it is night in the big kitchen, Tanga goes there to sit. The only light is the gleam of the appliances, the only sound is their hum. She sits on the bar stool. Sometimes she drinks a bottle of beer or smokes One of My Special Cigarettes. Her time in the Rogers' house has made her more attractive. Her cheeks are less hollow. Her eyes no longer dart defensively.

Joe has never asked Tanga to do the cooking, but she likes the big kitchen. It is hers now. The whole house is hers, even the soft side of the big bed when she wants it. She ruminates on her unlikely path to good fortune as she stirs the saucepan of *halpa*.

Halpa is one can of sloppy-joe starter, one jar of alfredo sauce, and a half bottle of Tabasco. Tanga invented it when she was a runaway girl in New York, stealing jars from bodegas and writing utopian journal entries about a land called Malanesia.

Junk Food

A few feet away from the incubator, the nurses talked through the night. Fair enough. The young mother had had jobs that involved a lot of sitting around. You talked to your coworkers about anything that crossed your mind. When you worked a job like that, the hours were there for filling.

Tonight the subject was ghosts: were they real, whose uncle's friend had seen one in the woods. The redhead claimed a creepy feeling overtook her in the old brick wing of the hospital. The black nurse was unimpressed. Ghosts, if they were real, wouldn't like hospitals any more than the living who miserably pace the waiting rooms or languish in the beds. Hospitals are the boring part of death. The monotony broken only by bedsores. The final proof that all life is waiting around for the last bad news. Now what were they going to have for lunch? Thai truck, said the redhead. Drunken noodles.

It was time to pump milk. She did this using a pair of plastic funnels attached to a groaning machine. As she pressed the funnels into her breasts, she stared at the baby. Because of the hormones, this was supposed to help.

The baby beeped, or, rather, its designated machines did. The beeping escalated and was accompanied by a flashing light. Every time this happened, the young mother gasped, but the nurses finished talking before one of them came to check. He'd probably just pulled a sensor. Could it be, mused the redhead, that UFOs were actually ghosts, souls that could go no higher than the sky? And was it too early in their shift for a Diet Coke?

The young mother had an overnight bag packed by her husband, which he'd filled with socks and granola bars and a celebrity magazine because sometimes she treated herself to one if they were traveling somewhere to sit beside water. And it did help for a few moments, sitting beside the whirring incubator, after the nurses had assured her (not with words but with their swift, methodical handling of the baby) that the beeps had been nothing this time. A celebrity had lost fifty pounds and another, in a grainier photo, seemed to have found them. An off-the-shoulder purple gown looked better on a reality star who'd once thrown up on national television than on the starlet who played Anna Karenina on cable. The magazine was a fix of the silly but vibrant world beyond the hospital. For a moment, the young mother felt superiority, for she had bigger things to care about. Then she was sorry that this was so.

When this shift was over, the nurses would have three days off. Perhaps this made them less attentive than the day crew. They spoke of what they would cook for dinner, and how, and to what extent it would confirm or thwart their weight loss plans.

The baby had a fever. Everyone acted like he pretty much deserved it.

You could smear chicken tenders with marmalade, then dredge them in flour and oatmeal. You baked them. They were low fat. What makes them crispy? asked the young nurse with the ponytail, the one who spent most of the night studying for some kind of certification she lacked. You use that spray. The young nurse had heard that that spray wasn't really low caloric if you held down the nozzle too long. *None of the tricks work.* The black nurse was thinking of joining Weight Watchers again. *You shouldn't; they just take your money.* I know, but for me it's the only thing. I gotta feel like someone's watching.

She couldn't get enough of staring at the baby, of course, that goes without saying, but around one or so the young mother, feeling heavy about the eyelids, took out her phone. One of its infinite functions was her social network. A flick of her thumb stirred a flock of statuses, the latest news of people she liked, knew, or at least met at conferences back when she was traveling for work and drinking in hotel bars because she wasn't even thinking of getting pregnant. Online, people were upset about the charitable activities of a chicken sandwich magnate: some people were buying more chicken sandwiches in solidarity and while others had forsworn chicken sand-wiches forever.

Janet, a former co-worker she hadn't seen in six years, had forwarded a cartoon of a gun-toting woman with menstrual cramps.

The baby's breath was ragged, snarling. The young mother watched the black nurse's face during the 2 a.m. feeding for signs she was moved. The baby burped and the nurse congrat-ulated it. The young mother wished she had elicited the burp, that some of the congratulation might fall on her. Instead, she went back to the phone. It was an election year and people were ravenous for slips of the tongue and shocking statistics about polar bears and welfare queens. People were bemoaning the lack of a "dislike" button.

Did anyone believe in psychics? They must, or psychics would cease to exist. The redhead had had her tarot read once. It seemed like baloney, but having been told she'd come into money, she'd won fifteen dollars on a scratch-off ticket a month after the reading. *That's your fortune?* That's it. Also, there were some fortune cookies left over from the day shift's lunch, if anyone wanted one. *Cardboard. I'd rather eat the duck sauce.*

Long term, the baby was going to be fine. Probably. None of the doctors would commit to any odds. At first, the young mother read the internet, but she couldn't filter out the stories that ended badly, the conspiracy theory that the baby's condition was caused by prenatal ingestion of Diet Coke (which she had prenatally ingested whenever she felt draggy and sorry for herself). So she only went on the internet to see what her friends were doing. They were waterskiing with their siblings, their spouses were the best ever, their dogs had eaten panty hose but would be okay, they were stewing about public transit, they took their names off unflattering photos, they hated how they looked from the side.

They weren't so bad, the nurses. At times they were as nice as her husband told everyone; she kept having to hear his half of cell phone conversations: *Of course, the nurses are just great, just great.* Maybe she shouldn't have snapped at the fat one who kept running over with the privacy screen. Maybe she shouldn't resent their competence when they changed the baby or the way they personified his nonverbal protests: *Oh, you angry with me, little man? You think it's about time to go home?*

On her husband's shift, when she tried to take a nap in their car in the garage, they told him the baby had gained weight. Though this was a relief to hear (even secondhand), the young mother didn't dare post anything about it, for she felt a variation on the aboriginal notion of a camera stealing a soul. Tonight he did not look as if he'd gained weight. A web of veins showed purple beneath the flimsy scrim of his forehead. Too vulnerable.

If things continued this way (or worsened), the tone of her future would be a stark contrast to her past. She'd become one of those people posting health updates and growing bitter over the way everyone responded, which really wasn't fair when you considered how out of place tragedy was in the format. "I wish there was a dislike button!!" people would post, unable to contain the knee-jerk exclamation points that followed them across the internet like wagging tails. Her thoughts would become increasingly wild and tangled and uncouth. If the baby didn't . . . well, then it would be this way forever, her brain a lunatic asylum on an untraveled hill.

A debate over how to grill a perfect medium rare without cutting to peek led them back to the topic of psychics. Perhaps it was a sixth sense that allowed a chef to know a steak's best moment without spilling its blood. Excuse me, said the young mother, can I hold him for a little while? This was sometimes allowed, in spite of all the wires, in spite of the fact that tapping the baby's back in a soothing way threw the heart monitor for a loop. It was even sometimes encouraged, because the touching was thought to stimulate the production of milk. Sometimes the young mother did not want to exercise the privilege, because of the wires, and maybe, perversely, because of the milk. But tonight she did. She wanted to believe her touch conveyed maternal love, that maternal love performed some sort of beneficial osmosis. Please? Was the nurse displeased about the interruption? Her manner was professional.

The young mother used to post about cooking, priding herself on striking just the right note of self-deprecation. Now, flicking through one status after another, she wished she could fall through the little screen into the lives described. She and her husband could be making crude jokes with farmer's market zucchini while purchasing blueberries for a crumble they'd make while they listened to the internet blues station and drank so much merlot their lips were purple before the dessert left the oven . . . in fact, it would very nearly burn. Which was hilarious. They'd eat it for breakfast when they finally woke at noon. Which of these details would make it into her pleased, breezy post? She would be spoiled for choice.

She wished her husband were there, but only one visitor was allowed at a time. At her insistence, her husband spent nights in their house. In, it sometimes seemed to her, their old life. She pictured him having a glass of wine and chuckling over some reference to the eccentric innkeeper on their honeymoon and scooping up the last bits of a vodka sauce with crusty bread while British indie rock played on the stereo. Though of course he was not doing that. There was no one there to make sauce or inside jokes. They were both miserable, only separate.

I've lost my baby, said a nurse from some other wing, visiting the ward to gossip a little and inform her friends that there was a birthday cake in an upstairs lounge. The young mother came to attention, but it turned out that the "lost baby" was merely some teenager in love with a boy who followed a college football team contrary to her parents' college football allegiance. *Whose cake?* Some guy in a coma . . . wife brought it in for the nurses, I guess. He obviously isn't eating any cake any time soon. *Chocolate?* Vanilla. She said that was his favorite. Guess she thinks if she feeds us we'll take better care. The nurses laughed as if this could not possibly be true.

The young mother had no time to bake bribery treats. Her armpits smelled as if she works in the sun and never washes. Sometimes, when she feels as though she might faint, she staggers to the vending machine and purchases E-5, a bag of baked potato chips, or E-6, a large cookie with a grandmother's head on the wrapper. E-6 didn't always dispense on the first try.

It was time to pump. She didn't bother to ask the nurses for the privacy screen; no one else was coming in this late and if they did they'd be no worse off for glimpsing the young mother's nipple pulled purple by the suction cups. If they were coming to visit a baby in this room, the worst thing was already happening. She put the baby back in its box and stared at it while the suction cups pulled. Trying to trick her body into thinking that she had a baby pulling at it instead of the rhythmically growling suction cups. Rerr. Rerr. Rerr, like an experimental symphony by a humorless German modernist. Afterward, the tiny bottle of yellowish milk went into the fridge. As in the young mother's first New York apartment, everyone had her own shelf, some with more milk bottles than others. Some nights, the nurses' lunches were stashed in the back. Though was it still lunch if it was eaten at 3 a.m.?

Ponytail was the newbie. She was sent for cake. Three slices for the three nurses. *Don't let them tell you no.*

The young mother had not always wanted to be a mother. After college she'd lived in New York, working a thankless job in a cubicle maze, calling people to harass them for paperwork pertaining to their asbestos exposure. Some of them had gotten cancer simply from embracing these men when they got home from pipefitting for non-union wages, cancer from laundering their husbands' workclothes. She felt surprisingly detached from these tales of woe. The people owed her paperwork, not sad stories. At night, her life in New York was a glittering marvel. Her friends performed comedy or folk music or poetry on little stages; a restaurant near her apartment sold only rice pudding. Evenings might be spent in a bar in a defunct hair salon, a bar in a defunct church, a bar atop a skyscraper, a bar in a baroque nook of Grand Central Station. It was as if all of civilization had been cast aside in favor of bars and why not? Even the cubicle boredom was somewhat relieved by Janet who sat next to her, not a glittering personage to be sure, but a type then foreign to the young woman, a single mother from Jersey. When she was not on the phone yelling at or pleading with her son's daycare, Janet filled the hours with talk.

She asked to hold the baby again. She wanted his grapefruit-sized head against her bare chest. Because you didn't just love your baby with your mind and the cultural accumulation of the whole history of baby-loving, plus the dozen or so pregnancy pics and "can't wait" statuses you'd posted for your "friends" (and their "friends"). Those things might be overcome with the right kind of counsel. But no, you also loved your baby with your body. Feeling his cheek against your collarbone was like drugs. Watching him scream and squirm against electrodes and examinations called forth your tears like magic, whether or not you were the sort of person who ever cried in public.

The nurses were looking at the price of suites in Playa del Maya. The pool had a bar you could swim to. Of course, that meant wearing a swimsuit. Perhaps they would try that low-fat chicken after all. Perhaps they could persuade their husbands that it was good food. Had they asked, the young mother could've told them about the surprisingly affordable resort she'd gone to with her husband, just outside an Italian village that made pastries to celebrate Agatha, the saint who carried her cut-off breasts on a platter.

In an hour it would be time to pump again. She had not yet rinsed the nozzles from the previous pumping, for doing so required going near the nurses to the pedal-operated sink. She didn't want them to see whether she used too much or too little soap. Plus, she would have to put down the baby, who just then was making adorable snuffling noises against her chest as if he cared about something besides eating.

As she almost drifted to sleep she was unguarded against a longing to be at some great, sparkling lake, wearing a swimsuit. She longed for the exhilarating faux indignation of being thrown off the dock by a boy, a boy not her husband, any boy who was that age, only she would be that age too, in the bikini. She blinked awake and chided herself for fantasizing escape. You have been thrown in the lake, she told herself, only it is cold and deep and not at all amusing. The sound you want to make is not a squeal but a scream.

Morning brought no change of light to the interior room. Her stomach contracted around its emptiness and she thought about what she would next eat. She wanted Doritos, but the vending machine in the lounge didn't have Doritos. They had

something called Zoinks. She would probably have to settle for
"hot fries," which were like the mummified fingers of someone who had been eating Doritos.

In her cubicle days, her co-workers talked between brief
bouts of work. Janet's favored topics of conversation ran a not
very broad gamut from her son's eating habits to his toilet habits. She was particularly fond of recounting the 36-hour saga of
labor and delivery, an odyssey of pain that concluded with the
phrase "ripped from stem to stern" and did not pass over the
release of her bowels. It was Janet's conviction that *they* did not
tell you these things and that it fell to her to subvert the cam-
paign of misinformation that allowed vulnerable young women
to idealize the experience, to excuse their jerks from wearing
condoms in hopes of participating in the so-called blessed
event. *Blessed event my ass*, Janet said. *You don't hear a veal refer
to a saltimbocca as a blessing.* The single girl enjoyed Janet
during the long days. They were on a diet together, which
meant virtuous lunches of microwave popcorn and occasional
splurges at the Mr. Softee truck, giggling like junior high best
friends. But they didn't see each other outside of work and over
night drinks the younger woman would imitate the Jersey
accent to her friends, tacking "my ass!" to the end of any available declarative.

After the bad job she had had better ones, or at least more
profitable. She had traveled. When he was not yet her husband,
she and her husband went to Italy, broadcasting from there an
online album of photos that proved they were willing to strike
mocking erotic poses with statuary even if it meant being
chased by museum guards, game for strange new kinds of
toilets. And well fed. Many of the photos were of food. They

visited a mozzarella farm whose cows walked into computerized stalls whenever they felt like being milked. The stalls dispensed treats and massages while the udders were relieved. The young mother's pumping equipment was by comparison barbaric and without reward.

The nurses spoke of what they might eat if they could have anything. From funnel cakes and corndogs the talk moved to carnival rides that had frightened them. Roller coasters. The young mother tried to remember a time before this when she had been afraid. One August in Manhattan, a citywide power failure was briefly misinterpreted as a fresh disaster, terrorists striking at an unhealed scar. The then single woman, who had lived in New York long enough to memorize the subway map and short enough that she was still proud of this fact, realized that she had no way to get home. Come with me, said Janet, and she only nodded her compliance.

It was cold in the room if you weren't in an incubator. The baby was like a little comet against her chest. They were fine as long as their skin was touching. They were animals. Animals didn't get bored or nostalgic. His heart beat exactly in time with hers. The monitor said so.

She did not wish that she was in Italy. She did not unwish the baby. She was caught in the suffering of wanting to wish these things, wanting even to remember them clearly, and running up against a blockage of pain knitted from love and hormones. She wanted to go back to her younger self, looking at the sun-drenched countryside from the window of a train and sipping a Coca Lite and eating a cheap, sweet pastry fashioned after a saint's breast, wishing with a lethargic melancholy that she had more to care about so that she might perhaps write a novel or paint a masterpiece. She would tell that younger self that some day she would have a husband and a baby and the caring would rip her apart from the inside. Caring was a bitch. Not that the younger self could understand. It was too separate. The younger self took her pain in little cups and savored it.

She wasn't even a young mother, not really. She would be forty before this baby learned to ride a bike, if he ever learned to ride a bike. Janet had been a young mother. By the time the blackout turned out to be nothing, an explainable thing, Janet had herded her young single coworker right out of their office, down Wall Street, and aboard a Jersey-bound ferry. At her toy-strewn condo, they curled up on the microsuede couches and drank tumblers of anisette, the only liquor Janet had. They laughed at how scared they'd been, even though they were still a little scared. Janet heated alphabet soup on a camp stove and they ate all the ice cream in the freezer before it could melt. The son was at his father's and selfishly the single girl was glad, because that meant she could drink as much as she wanted and not share the ice cream and when she threw up in the dark at 3 a.m. Janet somehow found her and held a cool cloth to her forehead. *You're a good mother,* she told Janet, because that was a thing that worried Janet; they had spoken about it while drunk. Janet made shushing noises and stroked her hair. Later, when she had a big belly and took all the classes, the young mother would learn that shushing was good, that it was supposed to replicate the sounds and therefore the secure feeling of the womb.

The baby's heart beat with her own. Her arms were tired but she would never put him down. The room's many machines made shushing noises, and the young mother wondered if this was by design and for a moment felt warm toward the humane inventors of such machinery.

Someday you will be too, Janet had whispered, amidst her shushing. And the single girl wanted to object to the pity in her voice, but the hair stroking felt too nice, so she stayed quiet. It was more the kind of thing she could tell her Manhattan friends: this woman with this terrible life felt sorry for me, *consoled* me by saying I'd be like her someday, ha ha!

Janet was the only one from that old job who ever "liked" the young mother's announcements. Seemingly Janet was enthusiastic about everything her long-lost friend did, especially eating dinner and more especially (as seen in comments with multiple exclamation points) suffering from pregnancy symptoms.

She blinked out of a light sleep. It was almost shift change. The ponytailed nurse came closer. *What's going on with that heart monitor?* The young mother did not have time to brag that they were beating in sync. The nurse was yanking at the baby's blanket, following the white wire to the sensor. Which was stuck to the young mother's chest, had been transferred as she embraced him.

Move, Ponytail said to the young mother.

She realized that if the baby died she would need her husband to die as well. They would not be able to go on with a lost baby between them. It had to be all or nothing. That way, if she ended up with nothing, she could move back to New York, to some borough neighborhood near the water, so distant as to be only reachable by bus, so unfashionable as to be semi-fashionable. She would be the mysterious woman who wandered to the bakery for bags of ethnic cookies, always with a sad expression on her face. Always elegantly gaunt despite subsisting on sweets.

The fever is worse, said the nurse, her tone this time not quite neutral. The young mother asked, *Does it have to do with the monitor? Would a heart monitor catch something like that?* No answer: the nurse was calling the other nurses away from their computer, where they were searching for recipes for lower-fat cakes.

She realized this was bluffing. She conjured New York because it was a place she felt competent.

This time they told her to leave. Her presence, any questions she might ask, would interfere with their job, which was suddenly to save the baby's life. At any rate, it was never their job to answer questions. It was for the doctor to know and to enlighten, to be distant or even imperious in his secret trove of understanding. The doctor was coming for the baby now and he would not be taking questions. She'd dozed on a great pile of time and someone had stolen it from under her. She should call her husband. She should try and eat something. She should not stand around here, begging reassurances from people who had no focus to spare.

They took the baby to a room beyond the one she was in. The young nurse continued her inspection of the other babies, quietly sleeping, steadily beeping. The young mother examined her ruined fingernails for any stray fiber that could be gripped between her teeth.

The young nurse touched her shoulder, but there was no feeling in it, and her smile betrayed the many places she'd rather be, places she would be as soon as the shift was over.

Shots of tequila and hilariously bad decisions and tottering heels and best friends and lots of phone photos with lots of teeth. The touch was brief and perfunctory and followed a few seconds later by a trip to the wall-mounted dispenser of sanitizer.

Actually, when she was watching her figure, the young mother made excellent oven "fried" chicken. It was a two-part secret: paprika and gently crushed cornflakes. But there was a barrier between the nurses, still in the normal world, and the small bubble of hell that enveloped her. Across that barrier no chicken recipe could pass.

Was it luck or just deserts? This and other questions followed her down the hall to the vending machine. There were quarters in her overnight bag and she fed them one by one into the slot, fumbling slightly with her shaking hands. The E-6 coil turned and cast the cookies off of their perch, out into the gravity that made them fall.

Only Children

Erica is staying with us. Night four and we are having pizza for the fourth time. This pizza, like its predecessors, is in the Hawaiian style, aka topped with ham and pineapple. All of us, Erica included, pick off the limp toppings; that's not the point of the Hawaiian. The point is that under the pizza parlor's current promotion, the Hawaiian pizza comes with a free plastic lei and if the delivery boy fails to say "aloha" when you answer the door then the order is free. Erica insists on running ahead of us when the bell sounds. Though he lacks enthusiasm, that boy hasn't once dropped the line.

Over this feast, Erica demonstrates her extensive knowledge of dinosaurs. I take the opportunity to raid the fridge for carrots sticks and a splash only of pinot grigio. Alex gives me a look, like later he will tell me that I lack warmth. Which I probably do lack, but you can chalk that up to always being on the defensive, to not having our future securely in the trap.

"And at the last hole," Erica gushes, "a T-rex eats your ball and you can't get it back!"

Distracted by our silent exchange of reproaches, Alex and I are equally clueless to the meaning of this statement.

"Those are meat-eaters, right?" Alex tries.

"They don't call them that anymore," I say, demonstrating the relatively recent nature of my school days vis-à-vis his. "Now it's 'carnosaurs.'"

Erica's face begins to cloud. We've missed the point. Batten the hatches.

"But *Dad,*" she insists, "can we go?"

I stall for time by informing her of the distinction between "can" and "may." Alex fails to appreciate the diversion.

"It's near where Shana gets her nails done," says Erica, feigning soulful sweetness worthy of a children's cough syrup commercial. "So if she doesn't like golf, we could drop her off there instead."

I get it. She's segued from precocious affinity for paleontology into a plug for the mini-golf course. You have to hand it to Erica; she misses little. She has noted the way I get huffy-puffy when Alex breaks out the golf clubs and she has seized upon it as a gap in which to wedge herself. But there are still flaws in her six-year-old logic. She doesn't know that the appeal of golf to Alex (sun, leisurely pace, masculine banter) does not translate to eighteen dinosaur-themed holes in the sun-baked parking lot of the wholesale club.

I tell them to go ahead without me. Picture Alex dragging in from an afternoon of chasing balls among the sugar-crazed birthday-party-attendees. You always get stuck at the near-impossible fifth hole, beneath a pterodactyl that lets out a grating "eyahhh" every ninety seconds. Anyway, Alex will come home, Erica will crackle with sour-gummy-baby electricity, and

I'll be poised in the air-conditioned kitchen with a cool pitcher of drinks. We'll see what he thinks of warmth then.

"And before that can we get a Slip 'N Slide?" Erica adds. Alex has been delaying this request because we haven't been on the superstore side of town. Really he's worried about sun-starving the lawn. But in the end, the grass will be ruined if Erica declares it.

I can't wait to tell Jamie how he squirmed over his precious grass.

But perhaps the listener is not from this town and is therefore unfamiliar with the circumstances behind Erica's all-inclusive vacation at Chez Daddy.

Erica has accused her mother's new husband of inappropriate ogling and possible touching. The setup is straight out of one of those lady-channel movies: the sudden marriage, the little girl in her bikini always doing cheerleading routines and dancing with a live garden hose on the back deck, the solicitous but visibly sweating stepfather who suggests that maybe she ought to come inside and dry off. He stands at the sliding door holding open a beach towel the size of a bear hug. Erica has seen enough of these alarmist lady movies to know about wrong-way rubbing. Plug her in and I get ninety minutes of peace.

Except that if you know Greg, you picture that as he holds the towel he's actually blushing and looking over the fence lest the neighbors discover that Erica knows all the words to the milkshake song. Greg is a youth minister and looks the part. His clothes seem to have been purchased by a middle-schooler's mother, hoping for a growth spurt. The shoulder seams always plunge several inches beyond the end of his shoulders and, though tucked in, the shirt billows around the waistline. When he lifts his arm to massage Mary Lee's neck you can see straight down the sleeves to his armpit hair.

So why the hurry-hurry marriage? Because Mary Lee and Greg would never cohabitate without God's blessing. Technically, I don't either, though none of those glass-bottled bath oils by the tub belongs to Alex.

⚘

Alex and Erica decide to "make a day of it." One of Alex's more charming turns of phrase/habits. We made a day of it several times in the waning months of his marriage: picnics and long drives and hotels two towns over with an expensive bottle of wine to counteract the sleaziness, or at least to reinterpret sleaziness as fun. Nothing like that on Alex and Erica's agenda. He is taking her to a country store in the mountains rumored to have sculptured molasses candy and llama rides. Then Dino-Golf. Then, probably, Hawaiian pizza, which she'll be too full to eat, having already had candy and snow cones and orange-powdered cheese twists and even pizza, the very flat, firm kind they sell at wholesale clubs and concession stands.

I wave from the window, and as soon as the car is past the stop sign on Crenshaw I call Jamie. There is no conversation: merely time and space coordinates. He picks me up within ten minutes, just around the corner (to avoid the church lady neighbor and her ongoing tally of cul-de-sac traffic).

"Hey, gorgeous," he says, making himself blush. "What are we doing?"

"Re-con," I say, ignoring the compliment. Jamie and I used to date. A businesslike demeanor is the best policy.

"You want me to go by Mary Lee and Greg's?"

"Yeah. Fast and then slow."

We take the corner of Crenshaw and Poplar too fast and the back seat, which is filled with empty bottles and cans, clinks and crashes.

"Sorry," says Jamie. "I was taking the recycling today."

"Clearly."

We drive in silence to Greg and Mary Lee's street. A pink bike with tassels lies on its side by the garage in unmown grass.

"Looks like a pedophile's place," says Jamie.

"Erica's been bugging Alex for a bike," I fume. "What's wrong with that one?"

"One more pass?"

No need. No cars, front door closed: God's people are out among the world. I tell Jamie to drive by First Baptist.

Bingo. Rusty Bronco in the spot next to the handicapped spots. Just in case some cripples and lepers drive up, I guess.

"Park," I tell Jamie. "I'm going in."

"Well, I'm not. Fucking places give me the creeps."

"No," I say, "you're not."

Jamie's blond eyebrows come together in a frown, and the pink of his skin deepens. The look is less angry/disapproving than it is petulant. Save it, I think, I have legitimate church business.

One thing you can say for Baptists, they believe in good air conditioning (and why not? Alex is not the only well-off congregant who tithes here). The office feels great after the trot across the parking lot. Jamie situated the car way in the back where no one can see his "In the Beginning . . . Man Created God" bumper sticker.

It smells like the churches of my youth: cheap cleaning products versus old spaghetti supper. I perk up to what might be a heated conversation behind door number three, but just then the secretary returns from the kitchen with her microwaved lunch.

"I was wondering if Pastor Greg is in?" I say, mustering my best Sunday-school face. "I've been talking to him about getting baptized."

"Oh, well, he's actually a little tied up at the moment. Is there anything I can help you with?"

"Oh," I say, "hmm." Like maybe if don't see a reverend in the next five minutes I'll go off on another twenty-something-year sin streak, which would of course be on her conscience. "Can I wait around until he is available?"

The secretary looks guiltily into her steaming Tupperware. All I need to know.

"They're having second thoughts about backing Greg," I tell Jamie.

"Meaning?"

"Meaning they're probably in there firing him right now. Meaning he will be de facto guilty in the minds of the towns-people. Meaning Erica will be living with Alex and me forever."

Jamie asks if I will be back in the sterile pre-furnished apartment where I officially live. Alex gives me a monthly check for the rent to preserve this technicality.

If Erica comes to live with us, the old me will have to be killed off completely.

"Would sex in the church parking lot calm you down?"

"Don't be disgusting. I'm getting baptized here."

"The water'll probably turn to steam the second it hits your skin." He makes an evil hissing noise.

Jamie doesn't really believe I am a devil-woman, though it has been an occasional pet name with us. But he also calls me angel. I don't want to discuss the impending conversion with him; I will not be able to convince him that it is my decision. It's a constant struggle to convince myself.

"Can we swing by the place on Rogers?" I refuse to call it "my place." It has industrial carpeting.

"Nope. Feeding time."

Jamie always figures out some reason we have to stop by his apartment. I can tell it's planned by the fact the bed has been lumpily made. We are greeted by Gandalf, an aggressively musky ferret that Jamie swears has been de-scented.

"Look how happy he is to see you," says Jamie, taking the ferret from its cage and menacing me with it. "Aren't you, Gandy? Aren't you?"

"Just give him lunch," I say. "I need to stop by Rogers Street for the mail."

"I'll do it later and drop it off."

"You don't have the key."

"So give me the key, geez. What are you hiding over there?"

Actually, there are some boxes from my parents' house. Yearbooks and love letters and second-place 4-H ribbons, all of it potentially embarrassing. I'm not sure why I didn't just toss that stuff after Mom's funeral; she was the only person who still valued or wanted to reexperience the teenaged me, before I became so regrettably, in her words, "boy crazy."

"Look, if the rodent is sufficiently gorged, it's my mealtime too."

Jamie eyes the bed and gives me a pouty look. I wish he realized how disgusting that is on a grown man, but if Jamie realized half of what is disgusting about him, he'd probably have another girlfriend by now. From a friends-only perspective, I'm sometimes able to see these behaviors as semi-cute. Like how, after slaying a bunch of "avatars" in his online life, he will smoke a cigar in defiance of his apartment's drabness. I can just about respect that.

"Oh, you." I slap him lightly on the arm and allow him to make some sort of flirty retort about liking it rough in a bad British accent. Then he takes me to the Sonic and we have large chili coneys and cherry limeades with that rabbit-turd ice that crunches so well. I wear my biggest sunglasses to avoid recognition, but no deacons of the Baptist church are currently patronizing this restaurant where you have to eat in your car.

"Glad you're not dieting anymore," he says, mouth full. "I like watching you eat."

I sigh. It's so easy with nerds. They're grateful.

By the time Jamie drops me off, I'm in a hurry to get inside and throw up the chili dogs, so I toss him the keys to the Rogers Street apartment.

"Good luck, darling minion." I should explain that when my mother labeled me "boy crazy" I wasn't hanging out with scruffy lead singers or motorcycle dudes. I went after the student body president, the best tenor in the Episcopal youth choir, and both boys from my high school with Eagle Scout credentials. Gathered their virginities like pelts. Wrapped myself in their devotion.

"Okay," he grins like a puppy. "I'll get that mail ASAP."

Poor Jamie. He's earned a poke around my old boxes.

꒰ꔷ꒱

When they get home, Erica thumps dramatically up the stairs and slams the door to her room twice before howling like a tortured cat.

"She just fell apart at the ninth hole," Alex explains. He is sunburned where his hair is thinning.

"You can't think that you're going to make it all better with treats."

The thing is, I have not actually asked Alex whether he believes Erica's allegations about Greg. From the outset, he just buttoned his lips and started buying presents. It must kill him, though. He's always *admired* Greg, in this totally sick, self-deprecating way. Like his ex has been rewarded with this great, godly, second husband as some kind of payback for Alex's betrayals. It's very easy to label Mary Lee "good," but if you break it down, it's just that she wears ugly sandals and talks to dogs/babies.

Though I haven't managed to dig up anything very damning about her, either.

"I think she misses Mary Lee," says Alex. Does he expect me to fold a piece of bread over some peanut butter, pour Erica a tall glass of milk, and talk this thing through? I manage a nod with downcast eyes, and I offer to go up there.

Erica has worked herself into a very pathetic state indeed. Eyes puffed and reddened, she sits on the bed twirling a new Barbie by the hair.

"Nobody loves me," she sniffs.

I strain to hear Alex's movements downstairs. Every time Alex is not in the room I wonder what he is doing. That's how I know I'm in love with him.

"So what?" I say.

This throws her. The crying pauses.

"Everyone has to love you? Is that the rule?" Of course, I will have to retreat. Erica is too rarified a creature for tough love.

"My daddy has to. And my mommy." Erica has only recently reverted to diminutive parental nomenclature. Probably learned it from a sitcom.

"No, they don't have to," I sigh, "but they do. So you should be proud of that. You are loved by lots of people. Maybe you should make a list."

We go to the closet for the scented girl stationery I gave her for her birthday, which she has never used. The list grows quickly. This is a child who is loved by no less than four grand-parents, three great-grandparents, two parents, various aunts, and the student body of Polk Elementary. The page fills before we arrive at the sticky issue of step-love.

Not that I don't want to ask. I am a bad person and full of sin. I'm not just saying that so I can get my splash of holy water and my diamond ring. Baptist or no, I have long been aware that my biggest, most reflexive sin has always been to wish others ill. Sometimes for no reason. But believe me when I say this anyway: I hope he didn't do it. I'm rooting for girlish con-fusion over trauma. Like maybe she's just too young to realize her life isn't a movie.

The doorbell rings and Erica suddenly perks up, looking at me for confirmation. I nod maternally (something *I* learned from television) to indicate that, yes, it is most likely the pizza man. I'm sure Alex would've thought to call.

Erica races down the stairs and I follow at a measured, serene pace (the old book-on-the-head posture in all its glory). She throws open the door and then there is the usual anticipatory second, but this time, no one says the promised magic word.

I feel a brief twinge of vindication and solidarity with Erica; we've beaten Pronto Pizza into submission.

But Erica's jubilation is all out of proportion, and when I finish my regal descent I see why: Alex has not summoned eighteen square inches of industrial-grade mozzarella and pineapple to heal Erica's wounds. He's called Mary Lee.

Mary Lee looks up from the hugging long enough to say, "Hello, Shana." She says my name like a kindergarten teacher might, honeyed precision and zero edge. No edge to suggest the days she cried when she was told the extent of my relationship with her then-husband. ("She really didn't know?" I asked Alex. "She didn't even suspect?" No, he kept saying, the shock had been "very raw." But, please, the guys at the car wash knew. We'd been at dinners with clients, as a couple!)

"Come in," I tell Mary Lee. No honey there. It's not even my house.

The air goes out of the room; we're all in the foyer and Alex has on his churchiest expression, so I know he doesn't have me in mind when he suggests a "family conference." I repair to the front porch with a tumbler of pinot grigio and ice cubes. (I was trying to disguise it as lemonade, but I'm sure the smell gave it away. The wine has turned slightly after a week of neglect.)

There is a small toad on the front walk, and I toss a few pebbles near it, scaring it in one direction, then the other. It soon learns to ignore me, or perhaps it is paralyzed by shock.

Ten or fifteen minutes pass before the front door opens and Erica plops down beside me.

"Family conferences are boring."

"Really?" I say. "I've never been to one."

"A real snooze," she says, and I wonder if she picked that up from the way I described a recent zoo outing. "What are you doing?"

We chuck pebbles at the toad until it lopes off into the monkey grass.

"I think I told a lie," says Erica.

My heartbeat speeds. "Is that so?"

"Yeah," she says, picking up a thin stick and whipping it at the nearest shrub. "It was on my list. I listed Kurt Tompkins. He's in my class. He doesn't really love me; I just wish he did."

"I'm sure he's fond of you."

"At the end of school he said he was going to have a birthday party at Dino-Golf this summer. But I think it's already been."

"That's very tragic," I deadpan, though I have to admit, her story did bring back what summer was like for an only child, the only living thing in a world of grown-ups.

When the family conference breaks for the evening the following has been resolved: Erica will go back to her mother's house (tacitly understood to be her real home), and Alex will go there for dinner tomorrow for further conferencing (having exceeded today's capacity for dealing with real life). Greg has been called, and has agreed to sleep at his sister's house tonight and perhaps for the rest of the week. The decision to call for professional help with emotional or legal issues has been deferred.

When Mary Lee and Erica are gone, Alex sinks into the sofa and begins rubbing the bridge of his nose with his eyes closed.

"Everyone assumes he's guilty," I say.

Alex moans and flaps a hand in my general direction. He does this when I ask too many questions about our future or about Erica, also when his business partner bungled their taxes last year, sometimes when he has to choose a tie. It means: Alex has left the building. If you'd like to leave a message, don't get your hopes up.

⚘

Jamie is driving to Florida this week to meet up with a girl from the internet, so I am without a co-conspirator. I tell him it's no problem, that Alex is taking me shopping in Memphis and we'll probably stay the night at the Crowne Plaza, so I'll be pretty tied up too. Jamie must be experiencing some freak surge of confidence, because instead of launching into a moral indictment of Alex's money, he makes a cheerfully crude pun about me being tied up.

As soon as I put down the phone, I pull my foot into my lap and gouge at my toenails. Oops, looks like I need a fresh pedi.

The nail salon is abuzz. Greg has not gone to his sister's. His brother-in-law objects to having an alleged molester in the house with their children, although they don't have young girls, just two rangy males slathered in Clearasil.

First Baptist has officially asked Greg to take an emergency sabbatical and now no one knows who will teach Vacation Bible School next week. There is a rumor that he has checked into the Best Western by the interstate.

I waddle out of the salon flexing my wet-tipped toes and feeling a little nauseous. Suddenly, I really hate gossip. I want to just go to Alex's tastefully furnished little house (which is in some sense also mine, though less so every moment), turn up the air conditioner, and swaddle in blankets. But instead I drag by the parking lot of the Best Western. Greg's Bronco is there by the restaurant: fifty varieties of pancakes, no customers.

When Jamie answers his cell, I can hear a shrill game of Marco Polo in the background. Internet chick has a pool and kids.

"I've found him!" I shout. "And I'll give you a hint where: boysenberry, pecan . . ."

Jamie uh-huhs noncommittally until a glass slides between him and the squealing.

"It's good you called," he says. "I need to ask you something."

"The Pancake Haus! Remember?"

"Shana, is there any chance for us?"

The old Shana would tease, divert, minion-ize. The old Shana always had something warm on the back burner.

I decide to do the right thing.

"No, Jamie. Not really. Have fun down there."

Lies make the Baby Jesus cry.

☙

On Friday, Alex and I are getting dressed for the evening, dinner at the club. The food there is dated, but at least the cutlery is nice and there are candles. I have mentally built this evening up to be the week's redemptive moment, so naturally it is doomed before it starts.

Doomed by Mary Lee when she tears into the driveway and runs for the house. I can see the top of her head from the upstairs window and am surprised to learn that she dyes her hair, less surprised that the grayish roots are growing out.

She tries the door and, surprised to find it locked, rings the bell in a hysterical, unrelenting bing-bong-bing until Alex emerges from the bathroom and goes down to let her in.

Erica is gone.

"What do you mean 'gone'?" says Alex, using the exact same tone credit card people use when you tell them your identity has been stolen. This tone implies that the addressee is exhibiting such gross levels of carelessness that the representative is tempted to retire from customer service altogether.

Mary Lee is defenseless against that tone. She begins to cry. "I let her ride her bike around the block, and she did it twice, and I was sitting in the yard, and then the third time I was waiting to wave at her and she didn't come by!"

She looks really awful when she cries, like a refugee from somewhere that children are being starved and bombed and hacked to bits. No wonder Alex found it so hard to leave.

"Okay," says Alex. Basking in the expectant looks of the only two women he has ever slept with, he transforms his best self, his take-charge manly self. He divvies up responsibility (I am to stay here) and walk-runs to his trusty Beamer with Mary Lee trotting behind in her ugly sandals. Saddle up.

⚜

Generally, I prefer to work with a sidekick, but I drive to Greg's hotel in my lonely Honda because only I know where he is. *I might be the one who saves Erica.* I repeat it, out loud.

When he answers the door, he blinks at the light, and I can see that behind him there is only the paisley bedspread, the chunky television, the careful arrangement of his pocket detritus on the dresser. A lot of pennies and nickels lined up in cylinders.

"Aloha," I say, even though Greg lacks the context to get the reference. One of the few traits I share with Jamie is an amusement with my own obtuseness. "They think you've snatched Erica."

"I see," he says, visibly nervous. He is wearing a muted version of a Hawaiian shirt, maroon with olive leaves, the short sleeves drooping past his elbows as usual.

"Can I come in and check?" I smile. "Seriously, I could use a little A/C."

I sit; he doesn't. While I jokingly poke the pillow lumps beneath the sheets, he begins to lift and release one of his little towers of change in a cascade of jingles.

"Erica's missing?"

"You seem upset."

He looks at his feet. "I keep thinking someone must've hurt her, for her to even be able say these things. I wonder, if now . . . some person . . ."

"Or she's a liar."

He blanches. Suffer the little children to come to this guy; he'll buy whatever they're selling.

"Greg, do you have siblings?"

"I'm one of four."

"Then let me turn the counseling tables on you for a second. Like Erica, I'm an only child. And that's, it's not a syndrome, exactly, but it is its own country, only childhood. We have our ways. An aversion to sharing, a flair for the dramatic. That's why I'm . . . not a good person. No, don't. I'm not. That's why I've been seeing you about the baptism. And you've taught me that no one is beyond redemption, right?"

In this way, we fall back on our usual way of speaking with one another, despite the unusual setting of a darkened motel room. When Greg talks about the sacraments, his awkwardness falls immediately away. Alex is like this when he talks about investment strategy, Jamie when describing any of the cult media he's chosen as his own. A man is sexy when he speaks this way: Greg's tentativeness has been replaced with a rock-hard belief in a God who promises a big literal family who will meet someday in heaven at a kind of church picnic with really long tables.

I reach across the comforter and lay my hand on his: "I don't think I can wait any longer."

Still in pulpit mode, he says that he's glad to hear it and regrets that he is currently on leave from the church, but assures me that Pastor Dave will be glad to administer the sacrament next Sunday.

I let the tips of my manicure dent, just slightly, the skin of his hands, "I could die on the way out of here. I-40 is a river of fiery death and I don't think I can face it without the assurance of those people waiting for me in the sky."

Fidgeting: he's already so tentatively moored a wrong word could damn him.

"I plan to see you there," I say, lifting the nails, but allowing the fingertips to brush the tops of his arm hairs. "I plan on both of us being at that table. It'll be better then. Not so many of these earthly . . . obstacles. Just souls and love, right?"

I flatten my palm on his forearm. His rabbit pulse carries through the sinew and hair.

"How about the bathtub?" I say.

"The water's got to be blessed."

"Then bless it." My hand encircles, squeezes.

He can't stand the contact any longer, so he goes to the bathroom. I wasn't sure he would; all of this was a gamble, a high stakes game of what-if.

Now the water is running, and when I take a few silent steps toward the bathroom I see that he is kneeling on the tiles, testing the faucet's output for warmth. I let my clothes drop quietly to a ring around my feet, then step out of the ring.

When he turns to see me, he revulses and covers his eyes: "Shana, no. That's not how it's done."

At various points in my life, I have been asked just what it is I hope to accomplish by my actions. Usually, I just say *I'll know it when it's mine.* I don't say anything to Greg, though, just go rip the sheet from the bed and wrap myself. "I can't do this in those old clothes. Those are the old me," I explain.

"Well," he says. He isn't sure how to proceed and the thing I love and simultaneously hate about Greg is that he goes ahead and does the most polite, least boat-rocking thing, which is to look at the floor while I step into the tub. Alex tries so hard to stick to his most ethical guns, but there comes a point where he snaps, where he has to grab for me even though we are not married. Greg has not yet been pushed to such a point. It would be better for him if he knew where it lay.

I scootch down into the warm water and close my eyes, waiting. I can feel the sheet soaking, becoming less opaque.

"In the name of the Father." He manages a sturdy voice, though the cupped hand is shaking so that much of the water comes loose before it reaches my forehead.

"And of the Son." I'm getting totally short-changed on these scoops of water.

"And of the Holy Spirit." Now for the dunk: he puts his hand on my forehead and pushes back. If we were both in the deep, chlorinated baptistery, his hand would be beneath my back, lifting me out, but he can't get that kind of leverage here, so for a long time I stay under.

So much of church is pretending to listen, pretending to sing, your butt in tights falling asleep on the wooden pew. This is the real thing though. God touching every inch. The only sound is the pressure in my ears and the rubbery scoot of my hands against the side of the tub, as I brace myself, letting the sheet float open.

I open my eyes and see Greg wavering on the far side of the surface, terrified. So I bare my teeth in a smile, bubbles escaping up to him like empty-handed messengers.

And then up: the water sloughing off my breasts, which are now bare, reborn.

"Amen," I say.

In his suitcase I find myself a pair of cargo shorts and an off-brand polo to pull over my nudity. He holds open the door, and suddenly the outside world looks impossibly bright compared to the hovel of a room.

We stand in the doorway, me enjoying the feel of sun, him . . . well, I can't tell what he's doing. He seems to be looking back at the ring of discarded sundress on the floor behind us. And I feel that I am owed a more honest accounting of his inner turmoil: discomfort due to arousal or phobia of developed breasts? My hand seeks out the answer between his legs, grabbing around the folds of khaki so quickly that all he can do is wince and, like always, submit to what the Lord has put into his path. I release him, though for a moment my hand remains cupped in front of me, holding only sunlight.

⚘

Back at Alex's, Erica answers the door, looking expectant. As if there were more than a finite number of people who might arrive there.

"Aloha," I say. "Did you know that means both hello and good-bye?"

She hugs me fiercely. Children: where do they get this trust? Then she slaps me on the hip and declares me "it."

I chase her to the kitchen, where I designate Alex "it" so that he has to be the tired grown-up who shuts down the game. "Erica, baby, why don't you go up to your room for a minute and make sure the dolls didn't miss you?"

"So, I guess you found her." I pour myself a glass of wine. With the chipped ice, this time.

I barely let him finish his account, already contaminated with a seed of comedy that will one day sprout into the kind of story he could include in Erica's wedding toast: she was playing "runaway." They found her in the woods, telling stories of her sadness and bravery to the squirrels.

"I think it's disgraceful."

Alex straightens. He hates disgrace, though of course he's been shrouded in it since we met.

I've got the floor: "The way you and Mary Lee and everybody are just tip-toeing around."

"And what," he is ready to assume command, "do you suggest we do?"

"I *propose*," I say, leaning heavily on the word he hasn't used, "that we believe in your only child. I don't know whose side you're on, my love, but *I* am with Erica."

He settles his glasses for another weighing of the facts, but I thrust out my hand like a crossing guard: "There are things you've led too sheltered a life to know about, babe. But know this: *we* are not the bad guys here. Not this time."

"Shana, I just think—"

"Don't think. Know. Do. I have been there, Alex, and I am telling you that he is guilty."

Upstairs, I change into my own clothes before I go to Erica's room. Her afternoon in the woods has left her smelling of child-sweat and grass, and for once she agrees that she would like a bath, as long as she is allowed to use grown-up bath products and to bring along her Barbies. I line up all the good stuff on the porcelain ledge: the lavender oil, the rosemary shampoo, the natural loofah. While we wait for the tub to fill, we wrangle the dolls out of their eveningwear and plunk their perfect bodies into the rising water.

Dusty Hunting

You needed a good cover story for dusty hunting. These rural liquor-store owners were the most likely to be skeptical of strangers, but also the least likely to know that the old bottles in the back were sought after by hipsters.

"It's for my dad," said Wendy. "Alzheimer's. He can't understand why they don't make these brands anymore."

"Well, I know we used to carry it. Wasn't nice stuff."

"He's a vet," said Wendy. "Came back from Vietnam thirsty, if you know what I mean."

"You live in the city?"

"Unfortunately."

There were four bottles in the basement, still sealed with the green tax tape that indicated pre-1982 bottling.

※

At home, the husband was already in bed. He really was a Vietnam vet. Occasional memory problems appropriate to his years, which were more advanced than hers. A decade into their marriage, the disparity sometimes went unremarked.

She fit herself under his arm, whispering about the day's hunt. *Farther than ever before,* she said. *Way out there.* She wouldn't mention the unpleasantness at the last stop, not when she had such a haul. Worth seven hundred dollars at least. Dusties. She wouldn't even clean them off before she made the rounds at the bourbon bars. Wendy loved that last moment that the bottle was still hers, when the pale cocktail man reached for it with trembling hands.

At the last country store, the wheezing owner had helped her to the car with the damp cardboard box of Old Papaw travelers, bottles designed for the inner pocket of a working man's jacket. ("Butterscotch forward," said the bourbon guys. "Burnt corn finish.") When he saw her bumper stickers his lips pulled back over his canines. "Don't come back out here," he said.

The old husband sometimes clutched in his sleep. This was the hazard of being under his arm. He clutched her torso and she woke gasping. Once upon a time she would lie awake studying his sleeping face, the way the wrinkles twitched and smoothed. She would feel sad that he was caught in some past she couldn't know, and sometimes she would wake him up to recall him to his life with her. But she had learned that this waking brought more confusion than relief, so she left him to his dreams. Her own proved elusive.

"You even have a father?" the owner had wheezed at her.

⋆

Downstairs she opened the boxes to count again. Seven hundred dollars if she played it smart. One of the credit cards paid off. She turned a musty traveler in her hands. Her father had not been a drinker. At her wedding he'd accepted a Scotch to be polite to the old groom, and his face had gone all red. At the end of the night he told her that it was not too late to come home.

She held the bottle up to the kitchen light. Thinned maple syrup. Where was the magic?

⋆

A noise at the front door. Was someone jiggling the lock? Had she been followed? A man like that wouldn't come here, she told herself, trying again to sleep, this time on the couch. But what could she do if he did? A noise in the wall had her telling herself stories about all the benign things it could be, but other stories occurred to her too.

⋆

When her father said "home," she supposed he meant the condo he'd crawled into after the divorce, walls bare except for an old poster of the Rockies, hung too high. When she pictured him there, she saw him scrambling eggs, his head as smooth as a pearl on a ring of monkish hair. Every other weekend these embarrassing inept dinners, her eyes lifted to that poster, drawn to cragginess. She still avoided calling him; she did not like to imagine that room or his loneliness in it.

✢

At 3 a.m. Wendy opened a dusty and drank. A swift internal burn: sugar and char. A burning that could only be quenched with more fire. It swept away her memories and replaced them with older ones: howling and dancing, desperation beneath enormous weight, a gulp of night air.

When the roar began to subside she was out in the streets, trying to find where she'd parked. What was it she wanted with the car? Oh: to drive to the rural liquor store. The man probably lived in the house behind it. She'd rattle his doorknob. She'd break his fucking windows with a rock.

✢

She found that she was on the same block as one of her customers. What would the bourbon guy do if she sat at his bar sloshing a half-traveler of Papaw? He'd be curious. He'd want a taste. He'd want to turn it over and see if there was a year pressed into the thick glass. It could be good for business. She'd been letting him have product too cheaply.

✢

"Everyone *has* a father," she told the bourbon guy, struggling through the burnt corn finish to recount her day.

"Total jerk." He agreed without conviction. He hadn't taken his eyes off her bottle. He was a jerk, the kind of guy who spoke more loudly and slowly to her husband than to his hipster clientele. "That stuff you're drinking was made for guys like that."

"Maybe it was made *from* them," said Wendy. She drained

the last drops and, grasping the bottle by the neck, broke it on the zinc bar-top. "Butterscotch forward!"

But the bourbon guy, as he mopped up the crude jewels of glass, disarmed her with an expression both bored and vaguely sad. "Someone's going to have a hangover."

꩜

Back home she found she'd left the door wide open. But no one had come in. The stash of dusties was untouched. The dear old husband was still asleep. She had been so careful not to let anyone know that the treasure she sought had real value.

She took another drink, as a reminder. The world was full of enemies.

Forbidden Fruit

He waited many years,
building a world, watching
Persephone in the meadow.
Persephone, a smeller, a taster.
If you have one appetite, he thought,
you have them all.
—Louise Glück, "A Myth of Devotion"

IX

June was not the type to steal deliberately. She *did* love candy, especially the oblong green ones her third-grade teacher dispensed when you successfully completed your times-table quiz.

The day they did zeroes, everyone passed and advanced.

Everyone passed the ones.

At the twos, there were kids who missed an answer. If you didn't get all twelve questions, you had to sit there smelling other people's candy, and the next day you took the same quiz while the others moved on.

The candy was labeled "sour apple," but the color was nothing found in nature. When you placed the gleaming lozenge in your mouth, your tongue curled around it and your eyes squinted and in that moment your very self was subsumed in sweet tartness, tart sweetness, a state of electric green like neon in the veins where your blood used to be.

June was fine until the sixes. She took that one three times. Candy clacked against the backs of other people's teeth. Her mouth watered.

The tens were almost as good as the zeroes, just scribble all those circles and you were there, blissed out in the sour-apple zone while Sophie Ryan in the next row erased her answer to 7 x 4 so many times her paper developed a smudgy hole.

That day June's mother was late and she and Sophie were the only ones in the room when Mrs. K stepped into the hall to consult with some other teacher. "Quickly," said Sophie, and just like that she was up at the desk, elbow-deep in the sacred jar.

June would never have thought of it. She was a child who let her senses go blurry in periods of inactivity, a girl who rarely knew when she was called on what had just been asked. But she did not hesitate to accept Sophie's looted gift. And when Mrs. K returned their sweet/tart breath gave them instantly away.

Below the earth, an ancient figure considered young June with interest. He liked a girl with appetites.

XIX

The duck-fat potatoes were not often on the menu, because the chef had to stockpile the precious lard of every *à l'orange* for some time before he had enough to coat the roasting pans.

Not for tasting, he said, waving the knife at June on her first day. *Never taste.*

Out on the floor the customers who tasted the potatoes silenced their companions with extended palms, closed their eyes, drowned out the Friday night noise with extended mms and lip smacks as if they wanted to shut off every sense but taste.

The only exception was a regular the staff called Madame. She came in with rich boyfriends and made a great show of her delicate appetite. She ordered but did not eat. When June carried Madame's plate of rearranged morsels back to the busing station, she passed through a fresh salvo of mmmmms from table fifteen. A quick moment in the dark space by the kitchen's swinging door, fingers to lips so quickly no one could've seen, and then again, because *goddamn,* they really were that good.

Her left cheek was still chipmunk-full when she turned to see the god of the underworld standing astride the rubber floor mats, their circular holes full of crushed garnish and shrimp tails and dark water. His arms crossed on his chest. "Now you've done it."

"Done what?" Her voice muffled by the most delicious potatoes known to man.

"Eaten that which was forbidden. Now you belong to me, a month for each bite."

June was puzzled. Besides that trouble in third grade, she had swiped gum from the checkout line, flavored lip-gloss from the drug store, chocolate kisses from her mother's secret stash.

"Those were different," said the god. "You have come of age. You are, as they say, a grown-up."

June put a hand to her mouth to prevent the duck-fat potatoes from taking an outbound ride on her laughter. "I'm not a grown-up. I live with four other girls. We eat cereal for dinner—with our hands."

"You are of age in this culture. You have an automobile."

"I mean, my grandmother got married when she was my age. But it's not like that anymore."

"I am not proposing marriage."

She regarded him for a moment. He was intriguing in his way. Like a black-and-white movie star who always played villains. Still, June at this age preferred skinny boys who needed haircuts and other kinds of maintenance.

"Go away," she said.

"Very well." He narrowed his eyes at her. "Sin again and I shall have you."

She flashed him a sarcastic A-OK sign and ran to check on Madame's table, passing through the spot where the god had dematerialized.

"Did you decide on any dessert?"

"We'll share the crème brulée," said the boyfriend, his smile innocent of the spinach wrapped around his left incisor.

"That sounds delicious," confirmed Madame, who knew dessert only by the way it sounded.

XX

For a decade or so, everything was allowed. Beer binges followed by Monte Cristo sandwiches at 3 a.m. Day drinking. Shawarma from a truck. One-night stands. She slept with her boss and was surprised that her older coworkers stopped inviting her to happy hour. But there were plenty of happy hours, all over the city.

Construction workers whistled and she waved merrily back. Praise for her sweetness seemed rude to contradict. The clothes of the age were as frilly as meringue and as brief as a petit four. She spent money on candy-colored lingerie and plane tickets and unremembered bar tabs and she was often short, but it didn't matter as a nearby mart sold frozen burritos two for a dollar. Bean and beef.

The underworld god would appear from time to time, as on the day she entered the kitchen to answer the microwave's bing of completion and found his face superimposed on her reflection in the microwave door.

"This is not food," he said. "The gods dine on nectar and ambrosia."

"Those gods don't matter anymore."

"People don't choose their gods," he said. "The gods choose you."

"I'm flattered," said June. "But."

"You are surely of age," he said, his ominous expression tinted with petulance. "The nymphs were barely shed of their first lunar blood, whereas you—"

"I have an IUD."

"You tempt the fates. Your pride will surely lead to—"

"You know, in *this* culture, they use your name for a cartoon dog. The one that doesn't talk or wear clothes."

"Someday you will not be so young that your impudence is easily forgiven."

June popped the microwave door. Light bathed her burrito and banished all spirits. The creepy thing was, she knew she'd set the timer and heard its ding but, at its heart, her lunch was still frozen.

XXX

The man she did marry was not good at giving gifts; for her birthday he installed track lighting in her study. But even after June had stared long into the refrigerator and declared there to be nothing for dinner, he could conjure a decent pasta from odds and ends. He changed light bulbs the moment they went dark; June was the type to drive around for weeks with one headlight, ready to weep and claim ignorance to any officer who stopped her. This steadiness of her husband's was reassuring, except when it was an affront. It doubled her shame when she went too long without changing necessary filters in the car or heating system. She rarely flossed. She did not want to be this way. She got a new credit card and charged a procedure to rid her teeth of wine stains. The chemicals sizzled her gums.

Sometimes she looked for the reappearance of the god, but worried more over the obligations of work and fertility.

XXXII

The day came when she loomed over a bowl of batter, the beater hovering just at her lips, and it was that moment she became conscious of her adulthood. Here in this kitchen there were wedding-gift gadgets, whole-grain cereal, discreetly placed mousetraps, and, at the center of it all, the planet-sized belly, a belly attached to her and containing a half-formed daughter. Suddenly, she could not hide from the thing she was about to do.

Only one lick, she thought to herself, and said aloud to the fetus, "I'll call you Salmonella. Ha." No one laughed.

So into the sink went the beaters, untasted. She lashed them with bright green soap lest she change her mind.

Her craving knew no patience. What sweetness could she give herself while the oven ticked?

Her husband had stocked the fruit bowl, would pointedly eat fruit and comment on its flavor. *So sweet. Really.*

She cut a pomegranate in half and spanked it to scatter the seeds. A smell of sulfur came from behind her, and not from the oven.

"At last, I have come—"

"Nope," she said, pinching up the little red jewels. She was hunched over to shorten the journey from countertop to mouth. She did not turn to see him.

"Surely you realize the history of the pom—"

"Outdated. I do not consider this a treat."

When June finally turned he wasn't there. The smell of the cake was getting bigger, spreading out. She told herself it would be better, the finished thing, than when it had been formless and raw. A cake was an accomplishment, if she could wait for it to cool.

XXXV

Your taste buds change every seven years, her grandmother used to say, trying to serve some ancient and objectionable goulash. Now June was old enough to see the possibility of her grandmother's being right: seven times four supposed changes of taste. The cravings that had come with the pregnancy did not recede after Laurel's birth. She lavished butter on her toast. Until.

And so: meetings. She hated them.

"I never knew fruit was so delicious," said a man who'd lost his third set of five pounds. "Whenever I want something, I eat an apple first. Then I ask myself if I truly wanted the other thing."

"You don't?" demanded June. The meeting across the hall was alcoholics. They had doughnuts. She'd almost gone there instead.

"Not usually," the man beamed. All these people had the same stories: apples, steamed broccoli with lower-sodium soy sauce.

Every day June counted, but there were many things that were not worth numbering, like the crusts of her daughter's sandwich, the peanut butter left over on a knife.

The smell of sulfur drowned out the peanut butter.

"Ha-ha!" cried the lord of the underworld, "Now you've—"

He stopped midsentence. He looked genuinely perplexed.

"What?" said June. The crusts were still in her mouth. In truth, she'd put extra jelly on the sandwich to insure overflow onto the parts her daughter wouldn't eat.

"Do I have the right house?" he ran a finger along the kitchen counter and examined it. Greasy.

"MOM!" called Laurel from the dining room. "What's for dessert?"

The god rubbed his thumb and forefinger together until the grease was gone with a little puff of smoke and a smell like an extinguished birthday candle. "You really gained a lot of weight."

"You don't *say* that."

"Mo-omm! Dizzzzzz-errrrr—errt!"

He turned toward the next room. "How old is she?"

June grabbed a serving fork and lunged for him, but of course he dematerialized and she fell. Her heart beat with such ferocity that the bracelet she wore to help with her fitness goals credited her with six flights of stairs.

XXXVI

It seemed best to go to her grandmother for advice. June's mother was the type who took up new religions or exercise regimens whenever two-faced January came around. The grandmother, being old and not of America, seemed more likely to be familiar with underworld gods.

June asked if the women in their family were cursed, if they all experienced . . . unwanted visitations.

The answer was not direct.

In the grandmother's village, there was an annual festival in which people left little jars of honey for the dead in the cemetery. In fact, a portion of any celebration—wedding, birth, coming of age—was thought to belong to relatives who had passed on. You left a morsel of every dish in an orderly line atop the gravestone. You took the time to describe to the dead what you had brought, who had made it, whether it was good weather for baking or a good year for yams. You asked a blessing of wealth and fatness.

Fatness was beautiful in the village.

When the famine came, people began to move away. They would ask their old neighbors to tend their relatives' graves at the festival, but then came war on top of famine and soon those

who'd been left behind were stealing from the dead, unearth-
ing little pots of honey and licking them clean.

"My family was no exception," said the grandmother.

"Our family."

The grandmother did not concede the point. She had never
approved of June's father.

"The village is abandoned now," said the grandmother.
"Everyone who did not die became American. Those old ways
are gone."

Before she left, June checked the pantry to see if there was
anything her grandmother might need. The shelves were
deeply bricked with square cans of cooked meat, the expiration
dates in some impossible future.

In this sanctuary of metal and meat, she prayed that Laurel
would be spared from hunger and fear of hunger. Prayer was
a thing for ancient people, and June wasn't sure how it was
done. She mostly aimed the prayer up, but she added a corol-
lary for the god below: spare her and I will become the thing
you wanted me to be. It's not too late.

ℛ

June made a friend on the playground, a woman who clothed
herself in a material that was like sweatpants, but which
draped with the swooping elegance of evening wear. The
friend had done a lot of reading about the monstrous side ef-
fects of sugar. Her ideas about parenting were more coher-
ent than June's, and indeed her daughter was not sticky or
scowling like Laurel, but possessed a wholesome glow and
advanced vocabulary. June could not believe that a woman like

this would choose her. It was thrilling to meet her for lunch at the organic grocery store with the long salad bars. After lunch they would push their carts side by side, loading up on carob and kale and unadulterated nut butters, discussing all the theories they seemed to share. This was adulthood indeed: everything settled and figured, the safety of their girls practically guaranteed. Laurel's skin cleared up. And the grocery bill had only increased by a factor of two.

XL

As Laurel's elementary years advanced, she was not friends with the wholesome-looking girl despite their mothers' efforts. And so it was someone else's mother who asked June to sit down at her kitchen table that morning.

"This is awkward," said the mother whose kitchen it was. The kind of kitchen with a full set of copper pots hanging from the ceiling like a disaster in progress. June flinched.

"It is?" Her first thought was that Laurel had peed on their pullout sofa.

"I'm a light sleeper," said the other woman, a hint of pride beneath the apology.

"Okay," said June, who slept like the dead.

"I woke up in the night and I decided to come check on the girls. I'd heard something, I was pretty sure, although of course we have a security system."

June forced herself to look at the woman, even though there was a bowl of Halloween candy on the countertop to her left. Halloween! This was early December. And there was enough of it that no one would notice a missing peanut butter cup.

"Anyway, when I came in here, the freezer door was open and . . . and Laurel was sort of *in* there, almost her whole body, and she was getting at the ice cream."

"Getting at it?" June feared the woman had smelled her desire for the candy like a conspicuous fart.

"It has these chunks of chocolate. I think she was gouging them out, like with . . ."

"With her fingers?"

The woman looked down as she nodded.

"God, I'm so sorry." June choked back a laugh, as she often did when embarrassed.

The woman's demeanor suddenly cooled. "She's a very hungry girl. I thought you should know."

"You mean so I can feed her?"

"They have spurts, you know. Times when they need more. Forbidding things doesn't teach them."

June tried to summon the indignation her organic friend would've flung back at this woman. She would've thrown on her sweatpants caftan and marched right out of there, not before thrusting a peanut butter cup in someone's face and declaring that it might as well be rat poison, that in the factories where such foodstuffs were made, huge diabetic rats lumbered out into the open to die. But June could only say in a flat voice: "My daughter is hungry."

"Becky says it goes on at school too. Laurel tries to trade for chips and cookies. She asks to borrow money. When someone doesn't finish their chocolate milk—"

Stop, June wanted to say, but she was Wrong Mom and this was the protocol when Right Mom deigned to speak to her inferior. You listened to the advice. You nodded. You promised to do better.

You cursed your carob-eating friend for leading you away from the pack where you could easily be picked off.

June pictured Laurel at the lunch table, grabbing someone's discarded milk carton and tilting her head all the way back to get the lukewarm drops.

XLV

June ate low-fat microwave popcorn sometimes instead of meals. It took up a lot of space without providing excess sustenance. It filled the house with a near-butter smell. It kept your teeth busy. Your hands.

Sometimes, though, she ate a meal anyway, as a second course. It was the worry for Laurel that made her hungry.

He will come for you, said all the stories. The prince. The wolf. The lustful god. But young Laurel did not heed these old stories as she did not heed her mother. She knew June would do anything for her: drop her at the mall and wait in the car, reading some book. Spend all weekend assembling a Catherine Earnshaw costume for her book report. Melt cheese on toast and bring it to her at the television and pick up her discarded socks on her way back to the kitchen. June's sacrifices were more ridiculous than heroic. For a while, Laurel asked for more and more. Then she lost interest.

"Spare her," June begged the dark microwave. Then she hit the start button and watched the popcorn spin, waited for it to distract her with noise and scent and the promise of food that could be eaten hand over fist.

XLVII

June's grandmother turned one hundred, enjoyed her abundant zeroes for three days, and then died. When June told people, they did not comfort her so much as marvel at the number.

In her later years, the grandmother had stopped looking forward, and then stopped even looking around. She did not recognize her own hands and spoke only of her village days. She thought her daughter was her mother, and that Laurel was the family's incompetent servant. June she called by the name of a girl at school who'd died of high fever.

When she was gone all that was left were the cans of meat and the shame of those who hadn't often listened. The stories had seemed boring, but now they were gone and the wisdom they'd contained could only be approximated.

After the funeral, June's mother's house was crowded with people she knew from her many hobbies. Everyone brought trays and crocks and ate heavily, glad of the excuse. The talk was mostly of how good the food was in the mouth, and how bad it might be for other regions.

June's mother, who'd borrowed tranquilizers and washed them down with pinot noir, rambled about the corruption at the heart of Western culture. She tried to tell a story from Hinduism, about the baby god eating all his family's butter, a holy squandering.

Then Laurel passed through the room.

Her appearance caused a hush of horror and respect.

Though a teenager, she had the half-mast, purplish eyelids of someone who had seen much. Her weight was a small child's, stretched over a woman's bones.

People tried to feed her. They hoisted cookies to the tip of her nose. They took exaggerated bites of lasagna: "See? Gooood." They told her she was thin enough.

Laurel's smile was wan. Distant. Almost pitying.

"She'll be fine," slurred June's mother, eager to get back to her own theories about the inability of the West to conceptualize a plausible afterlife.

"Didn't Grandmother ever tell you how we're cursed?" June asked.

"Honey, the only family curse is in these hips," laughed her mother, her mood shifting with some unseen metabolic process.

June's husband extended a deviled egg to Laurel, and for the first time, June noticed a tremor in his hand. Emotion, she thought. Laurel accepted the egg and everyone, with various degrees of subtlety, watched her nibble minutely at the white before setting it down and exiting the room in the measured gait of a bride. Already, she looked like the queen of some underworld.

L

Several times her husband receded into the grip of death and it was up to June to retrieve him, a process less romantic than the old tales would have you believe. *Take care of yourself too,* the harbingers warned, and yet she did it the wrong way until her body was at the precipice of diabetes. A binge could push you over, the doctor warned.

As her husband's condition worsened, Laurel's disordered eating went from the main melody of June's suffering to a grim descant, like a sliver of glass so deep in the heel that it is not worth seeking out with the tweezers, the pain freshly noticeable only when taking certain kinds of steps.

Take care of yourself too, they harped, so June honored her next birthday (a nice, round multiple of ten) with a pilgrimage.

At customs she was delayed when a fat agent took his time searching the young woman she'd sat next to on the plane, brandishing his metal-detecting wand and making comments, his tongue foreign but his tone unmistakable. June braced herself when she was called forward, but he let her pass through.

ॠ

It was not true that the village had been abandoned. Those that had known her grandmother were gone, but some of the old ways persisted. Still, when June went from place to place, trying to buy a crock of honey for an ancestor's grave, she was told that there were no more bees. At last an old woman at a fruit stand realized what June wanted the honey for, and led her to a dusty display of plastic food. *Very easy like this*, the old woman assured June. *Not anymore waste.*

She bought a sack of native pastries. At the burial ground, the markers were cracked or falling down. June wondered if the war had come here or if this was just the result of time and the weakness of the local stone. The god of the underworld was not here.

"You must free yourself from wanting," her mother had said during a bout of DIY Buddhism. The advice had not made sense. She had always wanted her husband to surprise her with more thoughtful gifts. Stupid, for now she only wanted to undo his pain. She had wanted her daughter's safety, but now her daughter had been devoured by safety, locked in a place of control from which there was no escape. June wanted to be looked at when she walked down the street. She wanted the god of the underworld to at least try to seduce her.

And, in this strange moment in a strange land, she wanted to devour the lame offering she'd brought her ancestors. They had not blessed her. She sank her teeth into their pastry.

"Come for me," she whispered to the underworld. "In this defilement, I belong to you, and you must claim me."

The precipice, her doctor had said.

She leaned against a grave and felt the sugar massing inside of her, the power of making her own choice. She leapt from the precipice with cake in both fists.

LXX

Laurel made it through adolescence after all . . . and on the other side, the spoils of adulthood: a car, a home, a job she could do on her home computer. Her relationships were conducted remotely and her food shipped to her in calibrated packets. Her primary interactions were with the condo board, where she relentlessly upheld the charter, even though people wanted to plant tomatoes in the flowerbeds. *Where would we be without rules*, Laurel was fond of asking. And fond of answering: *Nowhere. Chaos.*

She had groceries sent to her mother's house too. June called on the phone to announce their arrival and offer confused thanks.

When her husband died and her fear for her daughter's survival ran its course, the resolution left a hole into which June's memory began to fall and dissolve.

She ate lunch several times a day.

LXXV

The home was built around a large courtyard so that the residents could see the sky without wandering free. The walkways were lined with trees, which, in the summer, budded and bent with massive grapefruits. Eventually the fat fruits dropped to the ground, untouched. The residents were not allowed to partake: the pumping of their hearts relied on medication, and the medication failed in the presence of certain citrus compounds. The residents begged their young visitors to taste the fruit. They loaded their young arms with yellow globes. The young looked at them and said, "Did you get this off the *ground?*"

June liked to sit in the courtyard. She did not remember that the grapefruit was forbidden, but she had never hankered for it in the first place. She thought sometimes of a peach tart she'd once had at a hotel restaurant: a layer of shortbread, a layer of custard, a layer of glazed fruit.

The absence of worry had slackened June's creases and emphasized her relative youth in the home. Men came to sit with her. They recalled their exploits, their works and purchases, for her benefit. The presence of men brought the women who outnumbered them, and they also tried to impress June, for one always wants the prettiest on one's own side.

They told of the things they'd done to run households: scrambled hundreds of eggs, driven hundreds of miles to practices. Children were always eating or practicing, *right, June?*

"I have a daughter," June said.

Yes, yes, there were many stories to tell of daughters and sons, the way they abandoned you for people they'd met on computers. Forming families out of algorithms, preferring them to you.

June was glad that Laurel was not old enough to date. Where *was* Laurel just then? She hoped she had not left her at a practice. She hoped she had packed her a lunch.

A grapefruit hit the ground near June's bench with a sound like an air kiss.

Such a shame, said one of the residents, and the others jumped to agree. It was their most passionate summer topic: all around them this juice-gorged bounty left to sit and rot. A sin. An outrage. Nothing could soothe it.

While they were agreeing in this heated manner, June got up and crossed the courtyard. She had seen the god of the underworld on the other side, sitting in a wheelchair.

"I found you," she said, kneeling before him. Then her satisfaction dimmed. "Weren't you looking for me?"

"Perhaps," he said. "I came here to be with the old."

"I ate your offering," she said.

"No one makes offerings anymore. The temples have no walls; they only frame the sky."

His sadness was more real to her than the complaints of the others. She had forgotten that complaint was a symptom of sadness. She had forgotten much of the empathy she'd gathered over the years. She was pretty again, wasn't she?

She reached out to the god of the underworld and touched his hand. Here was someone who had admired her when she was truly worth admiring. She wondered if her husband knew she was here with all these men, if he might be coming to get her.

"I am not the king of anything now," he said.

June reached above them and pulled from the branch a grapefruit so large it took both her hands to cup it. "Here," she said, "an offering."

The god of the underworld still had most of his teeth. He accepted the fruit, methodically ate its twelve sections (one for each month of the year . . . he did not mistake). As June held his hand, the god of the underworld closed his eyes to better feel the acid when it loosed the medicine's grip upon his heart.

Waiting for the Miracle: Scenes from the New Brochure

The halls of Grace Christian Academy are lined at various times of the year with shoebox dioramas: the fifth grade does space, the second grade does dinosaurs, the third grade, for some reason, does San Francisco, and the first grade does miracles. This year you could see G.I. Joe in the lion's den and Barbie the cured leper, though the official rule said to use handmade items, not toys. The rule was meant to encourage creativity and, at the end of the display period, to make it easier for Eli to sweep the unclaimed shoeboxes with their flaking tempera paint into garbage bags.

⚘

Eli's habitual expression was sometimes compared to Jesus's, if Jesus had, in the course of staring down from heaven, become slightly sleepy. His eyelids lay like a thick frosting over the top half of his eyes. *Chocolate* frosting, the kids whispered, when they spoke of Eli's skin color amongst themselves. Like a Hershey bar, one would venture, a glint in her eye. Or sometimes: like doo doo. But if one of them went that far, there would be an objector, usually a kid whose parents had voted for Mondale. *You can't say that*, the kid (it was often Rachael Mathis) would hiss. But even Rachael Mathis had to admit that Eli's skin color was different from her own, and that it had something to do with why he was a janitor, while they were children at a private school where all the songs about God's love were sung at top volume.

Miss Toon was the music teacher. She was young and petite, barely taller than the sixth graders, though she dressed like an old lady in yarny cardigans with lots of pockets. Her shoes had a squeaky rubber bottom like a great wedge of cheesecake, so you could hear her coming down the hall. Even with the bumper shoes she did not reach five feet.

The children loved her for that.

Also, they liked her for her holiday productions. She was friends with the art teacher, Miss Rutledge, whose name did not delineate her destiny as clearly as Miss Toon's, but who had wild hair and turquoise high-tops to recommend her. Together, Miss Toon and Miss Rutledge coordinated Christmas pageants that were a whirl of purple spotlights and fake snow and carols sung so earnestly that all the parents were made teary and grateful.

Then there were the gala holidays entirely conceived by the enrichment teachers: Grandparents' Day and Balloon Day, Pajama Day and Smilers' Day (a dental theme). For Tacky Day the children wore mismatched outfits and looped their fathers' old ties around their heads like Rambo. For Election Day, they sang Lee Greenwood and put ballots into a locked box painted with a sixth-grader's rendition of Abraham Lincoln.

One morning, Miss Rutledge brought Miss Toon a cup of coffee from her own thermos (not the tire-smelling stuff in the teachers' lounge) and wondered aloud if it might not be time to organize another holiday.

"I don't know," said Miss Toon. "Some of the regular teachers think it takes away from their classroom time. They didn't like Pajama Day at all."

"Sticks in the mud," said Miss Rutledge, pressing the tip of her nose upward like a pig's.

Miss Toon pressed the giggle from her mouth with her fingertips. She did not like to speak ill of their non-enrichment-teacher colleagues, they who breathed the dust of fiercely chalked spelling words, or stained themselves purple mimeographing phonics worksheets.

"We'll talk," said Miss Rutledge, bouncing from the room. Miss Toon envied that bounce, which was why she made an effort to drink the coffee, though to her all coffee tasted of sarcastic men's breath.

⚘

Eli's day started like this: before the first teachers arrived to claim the mimeograph, he mopped the bathrooms and stocked the tiny toilets with fresh paper. The boys' rooms took longer than the girls' because there was more misdirected pee. Eli wore gloves.

If there was snow, the shoveling and salting came first, but in Nashville there was more often the threat of snow than snow itself. Still, you had to salt if there was the threat of snow. It was up to the teachers to stop the children from picking up the granules, or to make them spit them out. In the kindergarten, it was a popular thing to have a few tiny "diamonds" in your jumper pocket so you could reach into it and roll them between your fingers, so hard they almost cut.

If he was sprinkling salt during school hours, the kids would surround him as if he were scattering jewels. It made it hard to get the job done quickly and back into the warm.

Dr. Bomar had worked late the previous night, and so Eli had not disturbed him to empty his garbage and was surprised to find the principal's office occupied again at the early hour. Dr. Bomar expected small talk from all who crossed his path, so after Eli had pardoned his interruption he said, "You're here early." He was emptying the little can now. It was about half full with crumpled papers and butterscotch wrappers, a banana peel that was starting to smell. Eli said he was sorry he had not gotten to it the night before.

"How are you?" Dr. Bomar said, looking up from the brochures he was studying.

"Can't complain," said Eli. Relining the trashcan was easy, because he kept a folded supply of fresh bags beneath the one containing the current garbage. One of the third-grade classes, upon discovering this, had made themselves spaceman costumes by poking out holes for their heads and arms. The teacher had apparently been out of the room.

"We treating you like part of the family?" said Dr. Bomar. No one had told him of the misappropriated trash bags, feeling the incident was beneath his dignity and might anger him. Mrs.

Todd was privately terrified, though she was a woman of many private terrors.

"Treating me just fine," said Eli, mustering a vague smile. He had a pleasing voice. A baritone that put Dr. Bomar in mind of "Old Man River." Too bad he didn't sing.

Dr. Bomar smiled at Eli's departing back until the door was shut, then returned to his brochures. No question the school needed new ones. The original promotions depicted Carter-era kids, their braids half unraveled, their pants plaid. Kids from the era when the school didn't have a library or an art teacher, when it was just a bunch of refugees from the busing system who could barely scrape together tuition. He went to seek out that Cynthia Rutledge; she had an art degree and he rather liked the papier-mâché dragon she and the second grade had made in the upstairs corridor, even though it was a fire hazard and he was going to have to tell her to dismantle it. She was just the person to capture in photograph the new spirit of Grace Christian Academy, a spirit of possibility.

※

If Dr. Bomar was in the hallways, the kids could scarcely be kept in lines. He was huge! As tall as the ceiling almost! Everyone knew he'd been a basketball player at Vanderbilt before schoolchildren were even born. If he wandered past the playground at recess, which he sometimes did (he liked ask the teachers and children if they were being treated like part of the family too) he'd give his signature thumbs-up and the kids would plop themselves down on his shoes, one child per foot please, and he could walk like that for several steps. When he was in that mood, he infused the school with a loving energy they all could feel.

If you were really lucky, Dr. Bomar would crouch down Indian-style (though he was still taller than you) and tell a Cletus story. Cletus was an imaginary redneck who didn't have good sense, good manners, or a true devotion to God. He was always getting into funny scrapes that proved this. Sometimes Dr. Bomar told Cletus stories to the whole school during Friday morning chapel and sometimes he tailored them just to you if you'd been sent to the office for acting up. Even if you were in trouble, a visit to his office usually ended with a butterscotch candy. He kept them in a cookie jar on his desk.

Which was not to say that he wasn't intimidating. When Tommy Hogan deliberately flushed Whit Albright's miniature rubber wrestling guys down the toilet, clogging it and causing an overflow, Miss Toon sent him right to the principal's. The entire class said "ooooh."

When Tommy returned he smelled of butterscotch, but he'd become the kind of kid who'd pass the paste without using it first. The others whispered that he'd been paddled.

Miss Toon knew better. That was the genius of a leader like Dr. Bomar: he set himself up as stand-in for God. The kids liked him so much that if he showed them displeasure they could only hate themselves. Miss Toon found this quality sexy, though that was not a word she would've said out loud.

At the end of music class, the kids were lined up and waiting for their teacher, when Dr. Bomar returned for Tommy.

"Just one more thing, son," he said, his faraway brow as

serious as a thunderstorm. He called the boys "son." He called the girls "girl." "Now it's time you apologized to Eli."

Miss Toon was not sure if he winked at her on the way out. He was married, of course, but the wife was surprisingly plain: a few years older than him with a bowl of hair like a monk's.

⚘

Miss Rutledge's art room looked out over the part of the parking lot used for afternoon pick-up. The final bell rang at three, but the station wagons started lining up at two or before. It was very important to these mothers to be first in line, even if that meant the total waiting time would be longer. With the day's last class fully absorbed in making snake-coil pottery, Miss Rutledge peered out at the gridlock of perms: some of them got out of their cars to talk to each other, some read magazines or filed their nails, some simply stared at their steering wheels in a state of permanent readiness. Miss Rutledge was not sure that she wanted to be a mother, and sometimes wondered what people would think if they knew. Could you be fired for that?

Behind her, a disagreement broke out between two boys who wanted to be the clay collector at the end of class. "Pause," said Miss Rutledge, pointing an imaginary remote control at them. From her closet, she brought out two jars of the salty homemade Play-Doh she made in the cafeteria kitchen. She gave each boy a fist-sized lump of yellow and of blue.

"Make green," said Miss Rutledge. The class gathered around. "Ready, set . . ."

"GO!" screamed the rest of the class.

The boys began frantically mashing and twisting the lumps.

Zach was the first to achieve a uniform shade of green, so he got to be clay collector. He made a ball of his own snake-pot remnants, then skipped about the room, slamming it into others' scraps so it grew like the Blob.

"Hurry up, Zach. We've got to get y'all back to Mrs. Jensen so I can hide from pick-up duty."

Miss Rutledge really did hide from helping with the pick-up line. She could make blunt statements about her most selfish personal preferences in a way that would make people laugh.

She could say, "We're not going to paint the snake pots because yesterday I wanted to watch *Wheel of Fortune* and talk on the phone instead of going to buy the paint," and most of the children would laugh, though some of this laughter was a nervous manifestation of confusion. They had not imagined that teachers had televisions or phones or couches. And their parents never spoke this way.

Miss Toon's room was on the back of the school, and at three o'clock it was not filled with children listening for their names over the crackly PA system.

"I think it should be Save the Turtles Day," said Miss Rutledge by way of hello. "Do you have any more Starbursts?"

"The girls took all the reds and pinks," said Miss Toon, bringing the bowl out of its locked drawer.

"I brought art," said Miss Rutledge, waving a stack of papers gone stiff and lumpy with watercolor. She took a Starburst. "What do the boys pick?"

"Mostly orange for UT." Miss Toon allowed her friend to hang overflow art about the room. The anthropomorphized notes and clefs that had previously decorated her walls were unquestionably lame.

Miss Rutledge smacked the waxy candy about her mouth as if air was required to lessen the lemon intensity. "So, turtles?"

"Mrs. Todd thinks that we should cool it till Grandparents' Day."

Miss Rutledge sighed. "Well, I didn't want to tell you this, because it's the kind of thing that bothers you."

Miss Toon's throat visibly wrenched. "Someone's getting divorced?"

"Worse." Miss Rutledge took a seat. "It's Balloon Day. Our Balloon Day."

On the previous year's highly successful Balloon Day, the children had been allowed to purchase bunches of balloons, each attached to a stamped postcard. They all stood in the parking lot with their dozens of balloons (even the less wealthy kids had at least one or two), and when the visiting fire truck sounded its siren they all released them and sang "Up, Up, and Away" by the Fifth Dimension. The sky was polka-dotted. In subsequent weeks, found balloons were tracked with pushpins in a map that hung in the entryway.

"It turns out that turtles in South America eat loose balloons," said Miss Rutledge. "I read about it last week, but I was afraid to tell you. The balloons end up in the ocean, and the sea turtles eat them and they get stuck in their throats."

Miss Toon put a hand to her mouth.

"And so no food can get past. It's like they have a balloon instead of a stomach. But the balloon can't digest and they can't digest it, so they die. And they're already endangered, of course."

"Our beautiful balloons," said Miss Toon, tearing up.

"So sort of as an apology to the universe or whatever, we should do a Save the Turtles Day. I've got some art projects in mind and they could sing . . . I don't know, 'So Happy Together'?"

"Can I be alone for a minute?"

"Just think about it, okay?" Miss Rutledge was leaving, but stopped in the doorway. "Spoke to Dr. B this morning. He wants more photo ops. Picture it: I'll have them all paint their own shells, then we'll get some green sweatsuits . . . okay, no, I'm going. But think."

When Miss Rutledge was gone, Miss Toon went into the instrument closet and cried for the turtles. She was baffled by her sadness; she'd always been sympathetic, always had pangs, but now the sight of the jingle bell sticks filled her with a feeling of being very far from happiness, maybe even from God. She shook the bells, but they sent no shiver of Christmas through her veins.

At night she used to lull herself with the fantasy that she was Sleeping Beauty, that sleep was a pleasant interlude that made the waiting shorter. Lately the fantasy shamed her. As did the dates with the young men at her church. Younger than her, lately, they looked at her like a wrapped candy, knowing very well that she wouldn't circulate in that dating milieu if she weren't a virgin. And even though they were good boys who were probably waiting too, she couldn't forgive them for looking at her that way.

A miracle was needed. Only a miracle could have brought that monk-headed woman a Dr. Bomar. She must have prayed hard. And so Miss Toon prayed hard too, and in a few minutes she was able to return to her desk and begin transposing Amy Grant's "El Shaddai" into a more singable key.

It was only dimly understood that things were different in public schools. The only emissary from that world was Rachael Mathis, a sixth-grader who'd spent the first half of her elementary career in a school whose two main features were the hot reconstituted eggs served every morning and the 80 percent success rate teaching kindergartners to wash their hands after they used the bathroom.

Rachael's sentences often began with the shrill refrain "In public school . . ."

"In public school, they don't sing Christmas songs."

"In public school, the pizza is square and the sauce is really ketchup."

"In public school, you don't even have to know fractions."

Teachers were quick to step in and say never mind, she'd made it here now. Students rolled their eyes. Except Miranda Tate, who was not ashamed to share her turn at the class computer with Rachael, even if Rachael was a little bossy about how many pounds of computerized flour they should buy for their computerized old-timey wagon trip to Oregon. This was tantamount to best friendship in sixth-grade circles.

It was Miranda Tate who next knocked on Miss Toon's door. She was staying late, banging erasers for some of the teachers. Did Miss Toon have any erasers that needed banging?

Miss Toon pretended to look around, but she rarely used the board. She didn't like touching chalk. "I'm sorry, Miranda. Mine are clean."

She'd done a segment of her student teaching at a middle school, and it was her idea of hell. A group of heavily made up girls sat on a bench by the front door chugging Diet Cokes and yelling lewd things to passing boys, some of their vocabulary so exotic that Miss Toon had to make embarrassing inquiries as to its meaning. The sweetness of elementary school girls like Miranda was real: if Miss Toon wore a ribbon in her hair, they would wear a ribbon in theirs. They bobbed down the hall singing the Christian rock songs she'd taught them. They scrambled up to place their small, warm hands in hers. She was not sure she was giving them the armor they would need against middle school's sexualized cynicism, but she did not have that armor to give.

This thought almost sent her back to the instrument closet, but Miss Toon determined to master the rising emotion.

Many exciting things were happening at Grace Christian Academy. Mrs. Bart had brought in a Frenchman to visit all the classes and teach them to say hello and goodbye and thank you. (Amen had also been in the class plan, but it turned out that it was amen in French too.) Last week the kids had begun spontaneously clapping and swaying during a slave spiritual Miss Toon was teaching them ("Shut De Do"), and though at first it might have started as a joke by that naughty Tommy Hogan, soon they were all doing it and she could feel the Holy Spirit in the room. And of course there was the possibility of a new holiday, which meant weeks of singing to herself in the shower and the car, trying to get lyrics and arrangements just right so that after the letdown of the actual performance, she had compliments to bolster her. If Dr. Bomar had approved it, there was hardly a higher power than that.

᳐ᡱ

Miranda did not care that her best friend Rachael had messy pigtails and high-water corduroys, or at least she did not care in a way that made her less drawn to Rachael. Quite the opposite, Rachael's appearance, her shrill insistence on being heard when no one wanted to listen, her failure to grasp fractions, were all traits that made Rachael "the least of these." And Jesus had specifically said to befriend the least of these.

Slightly more baffling was Rachael's insistence on standing up for Walter Mondale, who in *The Weekly Reader* could clearly be seen to have yellow teeth. While Reagan twinkled at you like he might have a butterscotch in his pocket. And indeed, the post-election issue of *The Weekly Reader* revealed that the president liked jellybeans, justifying his 191-to-6 win in the school's mock election.

Being friends with Rachael was what Jesus wanted, and that brought Miranda one step closer to what she wanted. Which was a miracle. She was probably going to public school after Grace Christian Academy; her parents had divorced and her mom's new condo, though depressing inside and out, was on the fringe of a good school district. Or at least an acceptable one. She already knew enough Bible stories to drive the family crazy at dinner, so while they felt the money on Grace had not been wasted, they no longer had private-school money. And there were less redundant items that demanded expenditure of the dwindling funds.

Miranda had heard her friend's horror stories ("In public schools, the bathroom floor is covered with wet paper towels and dirty toilet tissue and no one cleans it up") and was resigned to her fate. But before she left her happy, godly school, this place where the janitor had once spent an hour going through the cafeteria trash in search of her retainer, where Tommy had stopped teasing her just because Dr. Bomar had asked him to, where "Corinthians" had been a spelling world, she wanted to see a miracle.

♪

Tommy started the rumor that Eli kept little girls prisoner in one of the fenced-off sections of the school basement. He saw the evidence when Dr. Bomar made him go down there to apologize: two crayon drawings of deer frolicking beneath rainbows, plus Eli's personal keys (not the ones that clanked from his waistband and opened all the school's closets) hung on a chain of braided pink yarn, obviously the work of some bored, imprisoned, girl child. The rumor was not as sinister as it might have been, but for a few days it did replace the previous rumor that the off-limits basement contained a singular relic: the cut-off ponytail of an angel, a hank of gold hair tied in a ribbon, hidden in the snarl of legless chairs Dr. Bomar refused to throw away.

♪

Miss Toon continued to sit at her desk until the windows, which looked out on the tetherball end of the playground, darkened into mirrors of the room, showing her to be a tiny apparition behind a teacher-sized desk, a child pretending to fill size-eight pumps. So intent was she on the lonely image that when the door swung suddenly open she screamed, irrationally sure it had happened only in the reflection.

Eli didn't scream back, but his eyes did look more open than usual. His lips parted slightly, searching for words. The day's final tasks rarely involved interaction.

"Sorry!" she blurted, a trace of scream still in her voice. She thought of how it used to be in the south, that a black man could be killed for happening upon her as he had. *To Kill a Mockingbird* was her favorite book.

"I bet I scared you more than you scared me!" she said, hoping with each new exclamation to detract from the original scream.

He nodded, gave his heart a little pat, and began sweeping the brown linoleum with his shaggy T-broom. She wondered desperately what he thought of her. Was she really as slight as her counterpart in the window?

"You're working late," he said. His only assessment of her, neutrally voiced.

"You too."

"Nah," he said. "I do this most nights."

"I put some candy wrappers in the trash after you took it."

She meant this as an apology, but realized it might be taken as an imperious request for extra garbage-emptying when Eli walked over to the desk, leaned down (just next to her lap!), and retrieved the squares of refuse that had recently wrapped Miss Rutledge's afternoon Starburst fix.

"You have a good night," he said, sweeping his way back out to the hall. "Don't work too hard."

For a long time she sat weighing his words, testing them for warmth, until they were so handled they did give off a tepid heat.

⚓

That night at dinner, Miranda Tate thanked God for Grace Christian Academy, for her teacher Mrs. Connelly, for her principal Dr. Bomar, for her art teacher Miss Rutledge, for her P.E. teachers Miss Dean and Coach Mason, and had not yet gotten as far as her music teacher when her father cleared his throat at her.

"One more thing," said Miranda. A foolish compromise: now she would have to choose between her music teacher, her best friend's trouble with fractions, or her miracle. She chose the last: "And may everyone who really needs a miracle please get one very soon."

"Amen," said her father, more to the potatoes than the prayer. Since becoming a bachelor he had learned to make only one meal: baked potatoes topped with canned chili and sour cream.

"Tomorrow we're going to learn French," said Miranda, who at ten believed that dinner conversation was a small, breath-filled balloon that ought to be kept aloft with merry thrusts. "Maybe someday I'll visit Paris!"

Her brother began to sing a song disparaging the ladies of France for doing their naked dancing where they could be plainly observed through a hole in the wall. Her father was probing a cold spot in his potato. As she sometimes did at trying moments, Miranda narrowed her eyes until the room became blurry, and she could picture instead the helium-filled balloons of the previous May (one with her name written on it in purple marker) making their way out of the Grace Christian Academy parking lot and into the clear sky like weather in reverse.

⁂

Miss Toon stayed late again on Wednesday, even though she and Miss Rutledge had come to no decision about Save the Turtles Day. She pretended to clean out her desk: the third drawer was filled with the tinkling remains of an exploded glockenspiel. Again, the darkness brought with it her slight reflection in the tetherball window. Again, Eli arrived to sweep the floor. If he found her repeated presence remarkable, his face did not register the reaction.

"You're working late," he said.

"Don't let me get in your way," she said. "Please pretend I'm not here."

He went about the sweeping: the usual whirls of linty dust, some pencil shavings, a pink zipper pull in the back corner. "You want to save this for lost and found?"

Miss Toon recoiled from the offering. "No, I don't think so. I doubt it could be reattached."

Eli pocketed the object. When he started the job back in the 70s, his pockets were personal space, used only to hold items like his cigarettes. In this decade, however, he did not smoke, and at the end of the day his pockets were full of refuse he'd picked up where no trash can was handy.

As an apology for not accepting the zipper, Miss Toon followed his progress around the room with a large smile that anyone could've recognized as a prompt, a plea even, for speech.

"These are second grade?" said Eli, gesturing at the watercolors.

"They're not very good," said Miss Toon, surprising herself.

"Cindy lets them use too much water. Everything blurs together."

"My niece likes to paint," said Eli. It was the most information-laden sentence he had spoken within those concrete-block walls. Something beyond the ordinary was afoot.

"Keisha," he went on. "She's got talent. Sings real well too."

"How old is she?"

"Nine. Goes to Moore."

There was no need to mention that had the parents of the young watercolorists not ponyed up the tuition for Grace, their children might've been in school with Keisha, forty kids to a room, maybe in a trailer rather than the squat brick bunker itself. The specter of those yellow buses, converging from the four corners of Nashville in the name of diversity, rose between them. Eli went about his final rounds. Dazed, Miss Toon swept a few glockenspiel tines into her purse and fled toward the front doors.

She was rattling them, trying to figure out the nighttime lock system, when a figure loomed behind her. "Some help, Miss Toon?"

"I was working late," Miss Toon told Dr. Bomar breathlessly as he demonstrated the door mechanism. "Miss Rutledge and I have so many ideas for the next holiday, we can scarcely sort them out."

"That's the spirit," said Dr. Bomar, holding the door open. As she passed him, she felt a brief but electric pat between her shoulder blades.

"Thank you," she whispered, more to God than Dr. Bomar. "Thank you, thank you."

Whenever Miss Toon was awake, her love shrieked from her

like the useless SOS of a lost cosmonaut. The signal was only ever answered by children who, like dogs, were receptive to a broader range of frequencies. But tonight she felt that her feeble vibrations had resonated against the broad chest of Dr. Bomar, had traveled along the thick wooden handle of Eli's broom. As she drove home she thought of the lights still on at the school and the men still working in that light.

⚓

Miss Rutledge spent the afternoon rediscovering the joys of the illicit cigarette in the mossy staircase that would give basement access if the doors at the bottom weren't chained. A forsaken kickball had settled on a drain, and Miss Rutledge gave it a teasing kick toward Matthieu, the Frenchman who'd given her the cigarette, but it was half-deflated and did not roll.

"*Matthieu*," she said through a plume, "*Bon soir. Fromage. Billetterie.* What words in English do you like to say?"

"I like this 'mee-maw,'" he said. He was not bored, she thought, by her company. "I spent much time wondering what it meant, this 'mee-maw.'"

The Frenchman had supposed "mee-maw" to be an American expression of desolation, having overheard it at the kindergarten drop-off point. Every morning, an older woman drove away, and this boy prostrated himself on the asphalt keening, "Mee Maw! Mee Maw!" Only later did Matthieu learn that it was merely a regional pet name for a grandmother.

Miss Rutledge laughed, thinking he'd meant the story to be funny.

⚓

Miss Toon did not generally leave her room in the confused half hour before the first bell; it made her nervous to be among the early arrivals who roamed the halls like a bunch of itinerants with purple backpacks. More than once she had been mistaken for a horsing-around sixth-grader by near-sighted Mrs. Baldwin, and even though she was not actually Mrs. Baldwin's charge, the steel wool in the woman's voice scoured her confidence.

That morning she risked it. She had invented a holiday.

In Miss Rutledge's room, construction paper hung from the ceiling in spirals. A collection of spattered dad-shirts on hooks waited to become smocks. Miss Rutledge emerged from the closet with two fistfuls of green pipe cleaners, "Hey, there. I was just hiding out, sniffing a little glue to get the day started."

Miss Toon let the joke, if it was a joke, slip. "I wanted to talk about the new holiday."

"Bastille Day," said Miss Rutledge. "We'll get Jacques Cousteau to teach them a song."

"I had a different idea."

"Lighten up! It's just a nickname."

Miss Toon took a deep breath. "Eli."

"Matthieu," Miss Rutledge corrected.

"I mean that we should celebrate Eli. He has a birthday coming up."

Miss Rutledge paced, considering. She twisted two pipe cleaners into a limp wand, which she pointed at Miss Toon's head. "Poof. You're a genius." As the idea gained steam, Miss Rutledge twirled around the little tables, conducting with the little green wand: "It's perfect. We'll have testimonials. A custom-painted ceremonial mop. Force the little brats to appreciate somebody for a change."

Miss Toon frowned. "I'll go get started on the songs."

Miss Rutledge tugged at her sleeve as she tried to go, "Hey, hey. I don't really think they're brats. Joke. Joking. Best job I ever had."

When Miss Toon had gone, the art teacher spoke to her construction-paper spirals. "She probably thinks I was really sniffing glue too."

In truth, she had been poking her nose into the paste bucket. The children had been buzzing about a safety video they'd seen: why would anyone would sniff glue, why would anyone accept powder from a stranger or get a shot on purpose? And Miss Rutledge thought: glue sniffing? Is that even possible? She liked to think herself experimental, but the paste bucket yielded only an astringent scent, a degraded cousin of peppermint.

⚘

Miranda was a good actress, and that was why she was chosen to tell her retainer story into the microphone at Eli Appreciation Day. Retainers, she would tell them, are very expensive. You have to take them out when you eat and if you accidentally take a few bites of your bologna sandwich before you remember to take it out, it does look sort of gross sitting there in the corner of your tray. And if a girl like Melissa Griffin, who dots her i's with hearts and who already kind of has boobs, starts making dramatic gagging noises (which only showcase her own braces, which catch far more food than retainers because they never come out), then you might be tempted to cover up your retainer with an unfolded napkin. And when you go to dump your tray, you might think it was just an ordinary napkin like you'd use to cover the little bit of mustard you had to spit out because your dad used the same knife to spread condiments on your sandwich and your brother's. Because he only has like two knives.

Miranda practiced the story in front of the bathroom mirror. It took a long time to get to the part where Eli is standing in the dumpster and you can't see the bottom half of his legs and he's tearing open these bags, spilling out milk cartons and one-bite apples and a slurry of pot-pie filling. Would be rude to take out her retainer for the speech? It made her words a little slushy.

Of course, Miranda knew she was not as pretty as a real actress. She had baby fat. But perhaps that could be the miracle—that the real her, the beauty created in God's image, would emerge, would finally be visible to everyone who didn't exist inside her.

꓾

The children had committed to the secrecy of the project with unexpected ferocity. One stood lookout at the door while the others rehearsed the Eli song, which was actually just an unlicensed adaptation of James Taylor's "You've Got a Friend." Eli could not be anywhere near when they sang the chorus, which required responsive shouting:

You just call out his name . . .

ELI!

And you know wherever he is . . .

ELI!

The second shouting of the janitor's name was not a part of Miss Toon's libretto, but she felt she ought not suppress spontaneous outpourings.

Of course, Eli knew something was afoot. He had been invited to that Friday's assembly. He'd been told he could bring his niece. It had been hinted that he might want to wear something less janitorial than usual. But Friday was two days away, two rotations of trash bags, two rounds of sweeping the classrooms, three applications of Windex on the front door's many hand smirches, and at least one round of pine shavings poured atop a first-grader's post-fish-stick sick.

⋰

There was always a lot of milling around at these fabricated holidays, and milling around made Dr. Bomar irritable. He pulled at his tie and cleared his throat into the microphone, his mighty Adam's apple squirming. Below him, the children flowed in crosscurrents and eddies. Miss Rutledge, who really ought to have spent less time showing the kindergartners how to draw a face atop their brown crayon scribbles and more time figuring out the seating arrangement, was running around taking photos with an enormous flash. Dr. Bomar had asked her to, of course, but her movements, her flash added to the chaos. Besides, the new brochure did not need glossy photos of kids milling aimlessly about, particularly not those fourth-graders staggering beneath unwieldy papier-mâché birthday cakes, still slightly wet. Dr. B did not like surreal imagery.

An additional ripple of disorder emanated from the second-graders, who were being introduced to a small black girl. They pressed in close, mesmerized by the hot pink beads in her hair. Keisha bore this with an expression very like her uncle's, her thousand-yard stare softened by long, curly lashes.

Rachael Mathis had strayed over from the sixth grade, a self-appointed guardian of the visitor.

"She goes to my old school," said Rachael, finally managing to capture several of Keisha's resistant fingers in a semblance of hand-holding. "Tell them how nasty the pizza is."

"Rachael, what grade are you in?" said Mrs. Bart.

"Sixth."

"Then I think that's who you ought to be sitting with."

Rachael walked as if there were a tightrope on the gym floor no one else could see. Some of her classmates in the sixth grade had begun to practice the brutal sorting instincts they would need in middle school, and Rachael could not be sure who would have her. Her best friend Miranda was up on the stage, practicing her speech to herself, lips moving.

They sang their song: "If the potty's flowing, and you need a helping hand . . ." Miranda watched Eli's face. He was smiling the same way she did when the boys told jokes that she was supposed to understand. When she wasn't sure if it would be better to pretend to get it. There wasn't much time to imagine what he might be thinking: in a few more moments she was going to have to adjust the microphone down to her height and speak into it.

For a prolonged moment, Miranda left the stage, the gymnasium, Nashville. Her nerves registered only two nodes of sensation: the cool damp of her palms and the circle of heat atop her left ear where her mother, trying to make her prettier for the performance, had burned her with the curling iron. She dissolved into the request she was sending heavenward: a miracle, a miracle, a miracle. And so she was the last one to notice that a fight had broken out in the second grade.

As Miranda contemplated her speech, the second-graders'

inquisitive overtures to Keisha grew bolder. A few of them reached out to touch the hair beads. Suddenly, they wanted a black friend the way they wanted the toys and cereals that filled the gaps between Saturday morning cartoons: passionately, genuinely, briefly. Someone wrapped his hand around a braid and pulled.

⁂

"Please," said Dr. Bomar, "you all are acting like a bunch of Cletus's." He huffed stormy gusts into the microphone, but there was no regaining control. His mind grasped for a Cletus story but could not find purchase: if he made Cletus a racist, he could never use him again to teach the children about saying thank you to their mothers or hanging their coats in an orderly fashion on the hooks provided. Panicked, Miss Toon began to play "Jesus Loves the Little Children of the World," and while some of the younger children sang nobly along, they did not know what was meant by "red and yellow, black and white, they are precious in his sight." They would've been thrilled to meet children the colors of piano keys. In their experience, children were mostly light orange.

Miss Rutledge walked into the midst of the screeching as surely as Shadrach into the fiery furnace. She took Keisha to the playground, where the girl sat on the teachers' bench and cried. When she had cried herself down to a few wet snuffles, the girl got up and walked over to the jungle gym. Without its usual load of children, it looked taller and more forbidding. Keisha climbed to the highest rung and looped her legs over the top. She hung upside down as still as a piece of fruit, her arms an inverted V, her braids just barely clicking against one another. Miss Rutledge picked up the camera.

Waiting for the Miracle: Scenes from the New Brochure

෴

By Dr. Bomar's accounting, that started a sort of miracle. Keisha's photo appeared in the new brochure. In a few more years, it was the 90s and the school actually had some black students. They were as welcome as anyone else to sit on Dr. Bomar's shoes and hear Cletus stories. But that was more in-evitability than miracle.

෴

For Miss Rutledge, there was something miraculous about finding a place to stay in Paris, so that she could finally afford her dream vacation on a teacher's salary. No romance emerged, but Matthieu's sister taught her to tie a scarf in a manner both chic and cavalier and became her pen-pal for life.

෴

Miss Toon did eventually share a kiss with Dr. Bomar, late one night in her classroom, followed by some vague groping in the music closet. It happened twice more before they agreed to pretend it hadn't; still, the incidents kept their consciences busy and their cheeks pinked for a long time. But that was not the miracle.

෴

In the Atlantic Ocean off the coast of Chile, a turtle circled listlessly. For days now, it had been unable to eat. From time to time it swung its jaw over a flotilla of plankton, but swallowing plankton increased the restriction in its esophagus without relieving the emptiness of its belly. It was no longer certain which direction was the sky and which the deep. When another of the listless rubber creatures drifted its way, the turtle did not remember that it was with such a meal that the trouble had begun.

And yet this time the inevitable failed to happen. The new balloon, a yellow one, lodged itself beside the blue one for only a moment. Perhaps the turtle took a fortuitous swallow; perhaps the properties of balloon latex have been neglected by scientists. With a rubbery squink, the yellow balloon dislodged the blue and both passed harmlessly through the turtle's digestive tract. In fact, when the heroic yellow balloon was excreted into ocean, its markings were still intact. Had anyone near had the opposable thumbs to stretch it out, he could've had seen that what at first appeared to be Sanskrit expanded into the plain sixth-grade phonetics of "Miranda" who did not dot her i with a heart.

The Dog Sense

During the night, when Leigh's extra senses were turned off, an inch of spring snow fell. Upon waking, Leigh understood two things immediately: one, that downstairs at the rear of the fridge, the rotisserie chicken her roommate had been picking at all week had finally passed the point of no return, and two, that in the night she had not heard her own car pull into the driveway, nor the keys plunked into the coffee can on the porch by the borrower. The after-image of the car seized her heart: its voluptuous cup holders, the big-eyed smile of its headlights and grill, the day her father handed her the keys, ten years after her childhood friends had received such gifts, because she had finally stopped partying.

That was when she remembered the third important thing: this was the appointed day for her monthly lunch with her father. The day they sat talking inanities over steak so that Leigh could prove herself still sober, still looking for work, still deserving of a monthly allowance. This allowance would be handed to her in the parking lot of the club, but not before he did his brief appraisal of the car. While he himself did not drive a compact and knew little about mechanics, he liked to kick at the tires and check the oil level, a proud but stern papa to the snub-nosed Civic. The little car had never disappointed him.

♪

Leigh casually cupped a hand over her nose and entered the kitchen. Karen was pinching threads of chicken from the carcass, humming to herself.

"I don't think that guy brought back the car," said Leigh. She took the previous day's sticky note off the fridge and squinted at the writing, as wavy as hair trimmings. The phone number she needed was indecipherable.

"That sucks. He was cute."

Karen parted the kitchen curtains and they both looked out. In the spot next to Karen's beat Dodge there was only fresh snow.

"Sucks," Karen affirmed.

Leigh nodded. She wanted to cry and rail, but found she was not enough surprised to do so. There in the sink was the mug he had used, and for a moment she thought the dog sense would save her, but no, all that remained of him was a smudge of mentholated lip balm on the rim. A hint of faux leather on the handle. He'd worn gloves. Technically, it was still winter.

"I need you to drive me around," she said, neglecting to apprise Karen of the looming bacteria crisis. Leigh simply didn't tell people about the dog sense, not even the roommate who faithfully submerged the dishes in neutral-smelling soaps, who accompanied her to meetings, and who possessed what was now the only means of transportation for tracking down the dirt-bag who'd borrowed the car in exchange for a greasy twenty.

"Can't. Never drive in bad weather."

☙

The dog sense had been with her for fourteen months now, one day longer than she had been clean. One minute she and her friends were ingesting unknowable powders from tiny plastic baggies, the next she was waking up on the floor, ultra-conscious of the mice nesting in the walls. She could identify the last meal of every body passed out around her, plus list the breeds of dogs they had petted in the interval.

What little she knew about dogs came from a trauma with a long-dead family pet. Not much that she cared to remember, especially now she could guess his experiences so accurately.

That first night she got truly messed up, trying to reverse it, but the part of her brain that had been switched on was permanent, and it was hungry for information. It parsed every scent in that crash pad into a long story, most of them unpleasant. When she was very near sober, she called her father for the first time in a year and wept that the phone conveyed only his voice and not his rich, pipe-smoke essence.

☙

A month after rehab she'd met Karen in a church basement. Karen was telling everyone about her bad choices with boy-friends, how her rock bottom came early one morning, her brain pulsing in an undersized skull, a holiday weekend in summer. She'd told herself she'd be okay as long as she stayed in this man's bed, warm in their mutual bad breath. First thing in the morning, he always split the last tallboy (it was a sacred thing with them, to leave the last one) into two cups and they'd toast and say "hair of the dog." It was the only time he showed no meanness.

Leigh thought then she wouldn't like Karen. She had never liked women with mean boyfriends and was fast growing an aversion to people who used canine idioms.

But that morning, the story went on, the neighbor's Jack Russell was yapping like it was under attack by the sky itself. And when the yapping woke the boyfriend to his own throbbing head, he thundered into the kitchen and took out a pork shoulder and a syringe. Out in the garage, he started injecting their perfectly good meat with anti-freeze. It took him some time, and afterwards there were bright green puddles all over the concrete. And then he marched out and chucked the pork shoulder over the neighbors' fence. The dog grew quiet while it ate. Later there was some mournful howling, but it wasn't nearly as loud as the usual barking. "And I didn't stop him," said Karen, blinking tears, "because I was in the house, chugging the last beer."

Beneath the ugly story and all its digressions, beneath her man's shirt that had come from some faulty boyfriend, a sincere sweat had activated Karen's citrus deodorant. Only the dog sense could read it: Karen meant well. She could never be anonymous to Leigh.

⁂

After they'd moved in, Karen turned out to be a person who delighted in money advice: stretches and workarounds and the fact that discounted yogurt didn't spoil just because the manufacturer picked some date out of its ass.

As well meaning as Karen was, she belonged to the degraded world, the world that Leigh had fallen into from the one where she'd been raised. When Leigh couldn't find work that suited her, it had been Karen's idea to loan out the car to people who had the odd handful of money, if never enough to secure their own wheels. This had gone well for a while. Most of the people were apologetic about their needs. They gave her crumpled bills or filled the gas tank partway.

Then this dirt bag.

He had been cute: green eyes, floppy hair, a smile in which unusually pointed teeth flanked the flat front ones. Someone who hung out with her ex Jason, which meant he probably sold poor-quality weed.

The moment he entered the house, Leigh had felt an ugly rising between her shoulder blades. When he introduced himself as Kirby, she felt his dishonesty like a swallow of stagnant water.

But she gritted her teeth, went through the motions, handed over the keys. When she could not stand his smile, she looked out the window, suppressing instinct. Following instincts had made her life what it was. How sure she had felt leaving school, loving Jason, climbing into cars with unknown destinations, even howling at the moon. And that was *before* the dog sense. The urge to howl had come from the party, not from inside her.

Almost every decision had been wrong. Though her perception now was preternaturally sharp, she trusted the dog sense no more than she trusted the party voices that still called to her sadness, offering to blot it out.

Since the sobriety and the new senses, she'd never failed to order steak at the paternal lunches. Rare. The blood spoke to her, made wolfish promises about how good she could be, how well she still might belong.

"You were the one who convinced me he was okay," Leigh said now to Karen, though it was not quite true. Certainly it was true that when Kirby was in the house, Karen let her kimono robe fall a little slack. It was the first time Leigh had seen her act that way, tilting her shoulders, giving away coffee and creamer. Always careful, except when it mattered. Leigh was starting to cry. "You told me if I did this thing with the car . . ."

Karen licked her fingertips and waved off the recitation of blame. "Fine," she spoke casually, though Leigh could hear the faster squeezing of her heart. "I'll take you. But we're going to drive slow."

Before they'd reached the end of the street, Karen had twice slammed the brakes and lost the back half of the car. Leigh cursed, her last remaining vice.

"We could go back," said Karen, and, with a resignation akin to kindness, "you could take my car to your lunch."

"You shouldn't loan your car to anyone you haven't known since at least third grade."

"Don't be so hard on yourself." Karen reached over and patted Leigh's knee. "I mean, what will your dad actually do?"

"Cut me off."

"Just like that?"

"He can be ruthless." They were on the main road now, where the snow had been mostly mushed aside by traffic, though there was still the odd ice patch. "I deserve it, of course. I did some messed-up things when he trusted me." The problem with being an addict was that you couldn't go forward without yet another accounting of all the wrongs. You had to hoist the pack of them on your shoulders before you went any distance.

"Addict things," said Karen.

"The usual."

"So what about the rent?"

Leigh felt a flare of anger that Karen had mentioned money; it was the only thing she hated going over more than her failure litany.

It was such a grinding bore being short of money. When Leigh used to go to meetings on the west side, the addicts would talk about all the adventures they'd had: shattering a crystal anniversary gift against a wall, assaulting the pool cleaner, sex in a stranger's convertible—it all sounded like such a lark, it just made Leigh hanker all the more for a line of coke edged with someone's father's credit card.

Now she knew which canned tuna was the cheapest, even though it sometimes had little scales. And so on. *Poor me,* she thought. *Literally.*

Perhaps she could earn some money showcasing the dog sense. She could join a circus. Tell people what they'd had for dinner and whether they were good. The problem was that people knew what they'd had for dinner. And who wanted to hear it if they were bad?

"You know you're an animal," said Karen, causing a reaction in Leigh so strong it nearly became a bark.

"When you're on your drug," Karen continued. "Your appetite overrides your humanity. Does your dad understand that?"

"He thinks he does."

"Well, you're not that animal anymore."

Leigh nodded, noncommittal. "Do you know where Jimmy Painter's is?"

There was a pause as Karen decided against lying. "Roughly. Never been there sober."

"We don't have to go in. In fact, it'd be better if you stayed in the car." There were always beer cans along the railing of Jimmy's back fence. It was still early enough that no one who'd crashed there was likely to be awake. Snow was so much fluffier than rain; it might not have washed away the lip prints. If Kirby had put his balm on one of those cans, she'd be a step closer to tracking him.

In the parking lot of the squat apartment complex, Karen seemed suddenly to shrink. Her fear of the place cried out to the dog sense. "Memory lane," she said, trying to sound tough. "It's funny we never ran into each other back then."

"Stay put," said Leigh. She ran around the side of the building where a few scant trees served as the toilet for a dozen pets, who bore the daily indignity of squatting there while the squirrels, smelling so delicious and out of reach, chattered down at them (and, to be honest, at her).

When she reached the rotten little deck, she found the curtains on the sliding door billowing open, and behind them sat Jimmy, playing video games in his rancid underwear.

Leigh mustered a sheepish wave and stepped inside. The little apartment was overwhelmed by its heating system and by a general masculine humidity. The only fresh air came from behind her. "Hi, Jimmy," she said, though people called him Painter.

"Leigh, right?" he said, though their acquaintance was long. When they were ten, having Easter brunch at the club, she'd happened upon him alone in the alcove off the dining room where the sundae bar sat between two green wingchairs. Instead of garnishing, he was tipping the whole bowl of maraschinos onto his ice cream. Wearing a pink bow tie and miniature seersucker.

"I'm looking for someone."

His furious clicking at the controller did not slow. "Connection?"

"One of your friends." She cleared her throat. The dog sense was suddenly so keyed up she could barely repress the growl bubbling in her vocal cords.

Years ago, Painter had sprayed the wall behind him with an anarchy symbol, though he hadn't got the slant quite right and it looked more like a top grade, circled for emphasis.

"Who?"

Don't growl, she chided herself, cramming down the instinct with the words, *don't you dare growl.*

Then an actual dog, a mottled pit bull, rounded the corner from the kitchen, its ears cocked to indicate it was on to her.

"You like him?" Painter dropped the drug-lord scowl and smiled with the joy of an animal lover. "Figured it wouldn't hurt to have some protection."

"He's a fight dog."

"I know, right?" Painter smoothed his hair back from a forehead that was larger than the last time she'd seen it. "This guy who owned him was into that stuff. Said this was the only way he could pay me. But he's retired as long as he's mine."

"He's been in fights," said Leigh, a gurgle in her throat. The dog had been kept hungry in a small cage, unleashed on opponents whose blood it could still taste.

"You into that stuff?" Painter was amused. He paused his

game to light a cigarette. "Out at that barn in Lebanon? Pretty rough action."

"A guy you know came over to borrow my car. 'Kirby,' he said."

"From Chattanooga," said Painter.

"Is that where he took my car?"

The dog advanced a step and Leigh retreated one, letting her gaze fall to the floor before slowly raising it. The dog bared its teeth as if to say, *I knew you were just a dumb bitch.*

"I don't have much time," she said, almost whispering.

"You're all clean now. Why don't you just call the cops?"

She considered this, but the truth was that uniforms often triggered the dog sense, and she couldn't count on herself to stay calm. The dog started growling again. She backed up another step, close enough for the curtains on the sliding door to hit her ankles when the wind blew.

Painter was going about his business with the video game, something with blond soldiers and Muslims, when he had an afterthought: "Hey, you have the title for your car, right? I mean, you didn't do something stupid like leave it in the glove compartment?"

"I'm not an idiot," and as the lie passed her lips, the dog began to bark sharply and with intent. As she slid the door shut, she saw Painter jump up to the highest point of his doughy sofa and flatten himself against the anarchy symbol.

"What the fuck, man?" he laughed, already losing his fear.

Leigh cracked the door. "Painter!" she said from the safety of the open inch. "What else about Kirby?"

"I don't know, man. He hangs out at Springwater sometimes. Dude, shut up!" This last was aimed toward the dog, who was barking frantically at Leigh, at the curtains, at the television with its blaring heroic theme, the pixilated hero shuffling back and forth while it waited for Painter to aim the gun.

Leigh's dog sense was not a psychic power, but the story was clear enough: the pit bull was terrified of his new owner's weakness, and he was an animal in whom terror had been married to viciousness. And there was Painter, laughing it off, mixing his signals, his pale flesh vulnerable and chemical-smelling . . .

"Painter, you really ought to—"

But when she pushed her nose through the opening, the dog started lunging at her again. The eyes said, *Bitch, I'll get my chance one way or another. And I will draw blood.*

⚘

"I don't think it's a good idea to go in there," said Karen outside the bar. "I just . . . I have this feeling in my gut, you know? Like it's saying this is a bad idea. Let sleeping dogs lie."

Your feeling is indigestion, Leigh didn't say. "I hate that expression."

But she knew what was in the bar the moment she opened the door and the few morning patrons squinted at the light. Nothing. The night before a guy had urinated in the corner behind the jukebox. Someone had punched someone else hard enough to draw nose blood, and the air still held a remnant of the fight's electricity. None of this was apparent or of interest to the morning crowd. Once the light disappeared behind the heavy door, Leigh ceased to be of any interest herself.

For a moment, Leigh forgot her purpose and felt the sadness of change. The Springwater was the kind of bar that attracted both dead-end drunks and freshly minted hipsters, allowing each to pretend to be the other. It was a place that had seemed so central to Leigh's identity that she could scarcely take in how little she meant to it.

The bartender, Abe, glanced over without recognition. He was busy receiving the flirtations of a girl who would never have spoken to him outside. Her many layers included a bright sundress and a man's gray cardigan. Before her on the bar she had a cup of coffee, a full beer, and a notebook to record her adventures.

And there, beneath cigarette smoke and lavender soap, a trace of the dirt bag.

"I'm looking for someone," said Leigh, and saw that the girl was prepared to be amused by her and her problems. "His name might be Kirby."

"Oh, *that* asshole," the girl said, talking to Abe as much as Leigh. "We were standing in the bathroom line last night and I thought we might kiss and I was *so wasted* I thought what-the-hell." She manufactured a large laugh, though Leigh sniffed repressed discomfort. "And he licked me. All the way from here to here." The girl indicated her chin and her temple. "And I was like *what in the actual hell?* Also, I think he stole my friend's phone."

"That's how he does," shrugged the bartender.

Leigh took a step toward the girl: yes, it was still there. The tongue swipe: swagger and corn chips. Then it was gone, lost in the signal coming from Abe.

Leigh turned to him. She'd never realized how rarely he washed his hands. "Do you have a pit bull?"

"Two."

"They love you."

"Much as dogs can. People always ask if I'm afraid of them. I'm not. They know when someone means well."

He kept them locked up, but when he came home they covered him in wet kisses. He shared his TV dinner Salisbury steak with them and they kissed him more, rivulets of love and gravy in his arm hair.

"It seems like everybody has a pit bull today," said Leigh, not quite realizing that what she was doing was starting the kind of conversation that idles pleasantly along all day. The kind of conversation that goes great with pints of cheap beer. There were a few crumpled dollars in her pocket. Before Leigh received them as change at the 7-Eleven, someone else had used them to buy beer.

"Always did have lockjaw dogs," said Abe, setting a napkin on the bar where he expected to nest Leigh's beer. "Never saw the harm."

"I grew up with beagles," said the girl in the summer dress. "They're supposed to be for hunting but what's crazy is, no one in my family actually hunts."

Leigh had met beagles before. She'd encountered one the morning she first woke up with the dog sense. He perched in the back of a truck at the corner gas station. His owner was filling up before a day out, and she had never felt anything like the animal's anticipation, which though it did not translate readily into words went something to the effect of *My God, he's taking me out! There'll be trees and dewdrops and fresh wet earth and little frogs you can snap right up for a snack. And through the undergrowth, the rabbit trail, the vector of prey, unspooling like a string that pulls you on and on, but not like a leash, sister, not at all.*

Leigh stroked one of the bills in her pocket, but just as it began to unfurl, a shock of polar air entered the bar. Karen stood in the doorway, daylight behind her. Everyone turned to glare at the girl letting in the cold, and pack mentality almost caused Leigh to snarl. But these people were not her pack anymore.

⚘

"Drive."

"You smell like that place," said Karen, accelerating into traffic. "Like a bar."

"Go back toward Nolensville Road," said Leigh. "Take the interstate. Listen, there's something going on with me . . ."

"You gonna tell me you've got a cold?"

"No."

"Because the sniffing is noticeable. Sniffing, sniffing, never a sneeze." She held up a hand to silence any response. "Look, tell me you're done now, for real, and I will believe you."

"I'm done."

Leigh felt Karen's faith in her fill the car, a drowsy vapor that made your ears lay flat, your eyes heavy. Of course, this faith was built on incomplete knowledge.

"You remember when we met, that night you told about the Jack Russell and the poison?"

There was no snow on the expressway, and Karen accelerated accordingly.

"My family got a dog when I was maybe ten. Curry. If she saw anything move outside, she would just go nuts, barking at the glass door. Squirrels, deer, kids selling candy. We laughed at her so much for that, like *Get 'em, killer. Get those bad Girl*

Scouts." In high school, Leigh was the only one home in the afternoon, and the dog's feeding and walk became her responsibility. And she often neglected it, sometimes because she was sniffing keyboard duster with the boy next door, sometimes because there was something really riveting on *Oprah*. The dog wandered the halls acting nervous, and it began to eat houseplants. Usually it was no big deal: there would be the unpleasant heaving sound, but more often than not Curry would eat the evidence before anyone else got home.

"But then one day she got to this little tree my dad kept in the office, and it turned out to be poison."

Karen nodded without looking away from the road.

"I felt bad for her. She wanted so bad to run around outside and all she got was being ignored and eating her own vomit."

"Dogs die easier than you'd think," said Karen.

"Not like I asked for another pet, but my dad said I couldn't have things I couldn't deserve, like he thought I was the only person in the world who didn't understand that."

They pulled off the interstate. They were back in their own side of town, and Leigh directed Karen away from the main drag, where the smells from the gas stations and laundromats and pupuserias were too assertive.

"I have to do something a little strange," said Leigh, already rolling down her window.

Mercifully, Karen's reaction was flat. People like her were accustomed to naked desperation.

With her head out the window, the north side neighborhoods hit Leigh with fresh, cold force. So many of the yards had skinny mutts on laundry lines, a winter's worth of their personal turds beneath the snow. If they turned around soon, they might just make it to the west side, where pet boundaries were invisible but electrified. Karen did not point this out, did not even glance at the dashboard clock.

"Down that way!" Suddenly the odor of the man separated itself from the smell of thawing dirt: the car was in the parking lot of the dollar store. From a half mile away she knew Kirby was sleeping in it, filling the backseat with boozy farts. Leigh pushed her whole torso out of the window, relishing the triumph of his rotten smell, urging Karen to honk the horn and accelerate as if the parked Honda would vanish before they could get to it.

They were in the lot and almost upon him when the airflow abruptly stilled and Karen was bailing from the stopped car, puking up rotisserie chicken and bile so intense it completely covered what Leigh had been tracking.

She did not need the dog sense to see him across the parking lot.

The man had climbed out of the backseat and was leaning against the open door squinting over at them with the annoyance of someone pulled out of a dream and into a hangover. Leigh started to run across the parking lot, but her tromped-down ballet slippers couldn't answer the wild call in her brain, a shock of ferocity, a need for headlong wind and the news it carried. When her feet slipped out of the shoes and hit the slush, she felt instantly how pink and soft and human they were.

"Leigh—" Karen's voice behind her was weak and fearful. She apologized between heaves.

In front of her, Kirby skidded across the hood like an action hero and got in the driver's seat. The door slammed and the ignition sounded. He smiled, not the cocky grin of his flirtations with Karen, but surprised delight in his private triumph. He did not glance toward the women as he put the car in gear.

⚬

His type was good at merging into the gray, and this side of town was gray even beneath its dirty snow. The Civic was moving away from them now, but Leigh held Karen's hair gently, patting and smoothing, as if they were just girls who'd had too much fun at a sorority mixer. Beneath the stomach acid and ruined chicken there was still Karen's earnestness, her determination to pay the rent each month for as long as it took.

"I shouldn't," Karen paused to spit, "shouldn't buy marked-down food, I guess. It didn't taste bad."

"Can't teach an old dog new tricks," said Leigh.

"You hate that expression."

Leigh was touched that Karen had noticed. In the midst of their indignity, the words were so perfunctory she hadn't even listened to herself.

"And it's not even true," said Karen, using her forearm to mop sticky ribbons of acid and saliva from her chin. "We aren't done. Get back in your seat."

The time for driving west had passed. The golf course with its untouched snow probably looked beautiful from the windows of the room where her father sat. Did he trust her enough that he would order their twin steaks, or would he realize instinctively that the pact was broken? This was not the time to think about it. Their quarry drove east and they pursued, yelping encouragements to bolster their small supply of hope.

Senseless Women

The facility took in a lot of sad cases, but not many interesting ones. Still, Miriam gave her superiors regular updates on the variations she observed: Mrs. Alden had moaned, Mrs. Bledsoe had a twitch that was almost a flinch, and, on one particularly exciting occasion, Ms. Bradford had barked out a note that was very like a laugh. None of them had opened their eyes. The doctor sometimes looked up from his emails as Miriam made her reports.

Dr. Salyer, who was in charge of the facility, had gone to med school in Bermuda. In his graduation picture, he wore a stethoscope and fluorescent pink sunglasses. When he briefed Miriam on the new patient, he had a new pair, black Ray-Bans, shoved up into his lustrous hair. "This is a little different from our usual bebop," he said.

From the moment the nameless patient had been brought to the ER at the university hospital, she had not stopped crying out. At first, it was understandable: the poison was burning away all of her wiring, the neural pathways from eyes and ears and skin. But even after sedation, she continued to speak and ask questions she could not hear the answers to. Once the meds had faded and the sutures were sewn and the machines settled into the monotonous beeps of life measuring, the patient continued to speak. It was unusual, certainly, but actually a little annoying in the overcrowded hospital, so she had been remanded to the long-term facility where Miriam and Dr. Salyer spent their quieter careers.

The other nurses didn't care about Bermuda or the sunglasses because they were all in love with him. Miriam had more professionalism in her pinky finger, but she felt no need to work at a livelier or more prestigious hospital.

"You should write it up," said Miriam. Dr. Salyer was flipping through the thin chart for the tenth time, looking for the name of the syndrome. "Yeah, right."

"Those guys downtown think they know it all, but they go too fast. It makes them careless." This was the only thing she'd said to Dr. Salyer that was not a symptom or, more commonly, a status.

"They think it could stop at any time. Her brain will just wind down."

For the first week, the Jane Doe repeated the same SOS: *I don't know if anyone is out there, but I am not dead. DO NOT PULL THE PLUG. Someone is in here.* The sort of thing you'd say to fend off an intruder from a bathroom stall. The patient had no apparent reaction when touched in a soothing way at the grey roots of her long hair.

Miriam didn't like the term "Jane Doe." She named the patient Lady Voice.

Dr. Salyer made the patient Miriam's special charge, since

Miriam was the only one who wasn't spooked by her. Miriam was accustomed to having more patience than most. She accepted responsibility for Lady Voice with a glimmer of feeling that was the closest she came to vanity.

I feel that I am talking, said Lady Voice. The SOS had apparently been deemed effective or pointless, either way not worth pursuing. *I can feel a buzz in my head that I know is speech, but I can't hear. I guess I'm trapped.*

At least, Miriam reflected, she did not know that she was at that moment having her soiled sheets changed. Then Lady Voice did something surprising: she laughed. *Hey,* and Miriam could almost swear she was being addressed. *How did Helen Keller burn her ear?*

It seemed polite to pause. Miriam appraised a stain on the sheet, a bodily ooze in a floral shape. Lady Voice clucked with anticipation: *She answered the iron. How did she burn the other one? THEY CALLED BACK!* The Voice chuckled. *I haven't thought of those in years.*

Miriam made rounds, checked vitals. In spite of what people thought, conscribed lives were also worth living.

On Miriam's next pass, the patient was still telling jokes, though she had run out of perfectly recollected ones. *Oh, it's something about ordering a whisky but they don't serve him because he's a piece of string . . . How would a string drink whisky anyway? Just absorption, I guess. Maybe that's the punch line? Like guys in bars are self-absorbed?*

Miriam decided to buy a notebook for transcription. Any of this could be important for Dr. Salyer's paper.

⚘

"That sweet man just truly cares about these patients," said Luanne in the nurse's lounge. "The other day, after we unplugged Mr. Giorgio, he walks up to me and tells me he needs a hug."

"Never find another doctor like that."

"Sweet man."

"He said there wasn't enough love in our profession. That we must never resist feeling love."

ℛ

When morning cast bluish window shapes on the facility's linoleum, Miriam's shift was supposed to be over. She was in the locker room, retrieving her cardigan and dirty Tupperware, when the lights went out.

The facility had backup generators; she knew that. Still, her heart seized.

The Lady's lights were on, but she was silent. Miriam ran in, hoping for something she couldn't name, but it turned out only to be a rare reflective pause.

He will come for me. I know it. I just have to pass the time. Lady Voice's mouth flatlined for only a moment.

God, there's so little to tell about most of my years. I worked in class-action lawsuits. Tracking expenses. Making sure the lawyers' sandwiches got subtracted from the big payouts. Those people had stories, man. These women had run out and got the very first fake breasts and they still ended up alone. Debilitated. Their daughters and spouses and friends had run away over the indignity of helping them use the toilet. They had to use a grabber to get a banana off the kitchen counter. Well, that isn't so interesting, I guess. There was this one woman who would always tell me about her grabber and her bananas. She couldn't see how many were left up there and there was always one straggler that went brown and attracted those little flies.

Drosophilia, thought Miriam, *lover of dew*. In biology class, hers had reproduced more than anyone's: three generations.

Miriam began to take her lunch into the patient's room. It was like having a very strange radio. She had to drag herself away, knowing she might miss some transmission that would never be received, never repeated. Here was a woman who had been poisoned. Silenced. And yet.

I am worth saving, she said. *I am loved. I haven't talked to my family in a while, I know, but they'll want to see me saved. And there is him. You, if you're here. I don't have to say your name.*

There were others, of course. You know those bowls of sesame cracker mix on the bar, and you eat it just because it's there? When I reached for him, it wasn't like that. It wasn't just proximity. This was love.

But I did have other options.

In high school, there was that kid whose dad owned the grocery store. All the grocery stores. Come to think of it, he did date my sister. Not seriously. She wasn't mad about that one.

Then there was the lifeguard . . .

As they progressed through the loves of the Lady Voice, Miriam realized that she was waiting to hear about the poisoner, hoping to get the clue that would solve the case, if there was a case. If she had to appear in court, she would have to buy a skirt suit. The poisoner would be in orange scrubs, glaring at her. She would try not to look.

Miriam recalled an afternoon as a child: she woke, not from a nap exactly, but from a sustained period of insensitivity—a time in which the world had not quite reached her. Then sud-

denly she was aware of tomato soup on a spoon, her mother
and sister talking at the kitchen counter. Her mother explaining that Miriam "felt things too much." It seemed an inade-
quate explanation for the lost time, which had proved, hadn't
it, that she controlled her feeling quite well. For once, Miriam
felt included in Renee's skeptical sigh.

It had been three years since Miriam had called her sister,
and she fumbled over the phone in the lounge, first dialing a
florist and then an exterminator before getting through to
Renee's cheery message about who all you had missed but
could leave a message for: Matt, Tristan, Chelsea, Bobo, Marlin.
As the old phone warmed, it smelled of toasted dust. All the
other nurses used cellular. When the message beeped, Miriam
blew into the plastic mouthpiece so that her breath became a
little cloud of static. "Hot date?" joked the nurse eating a cold
eggroll at the lunch table. There wasn't even anyone there to
appreciate the jibe.

*I wasn't always a legal secretary. At one point I was working my
way up as a production assistant in movies. P.A., they say in the
business. Gopher, my parents said, but it was more than that. I
worked for a documentarian. He studied monogamy in the wild,
following these Arctic foxes around to prove they mated for life. His
wife had left him for an actor.*

*The truth was they were mostly monogamous. They cheated.
There was this one . . . well, technically, they are called bitches, and
this bitch had a silver-tipped tail. She didn't have a mate and she
would just, like, get near the males and present: put her ass right in
the air in front of their noses.*

*Well, there was this one fox couple we were mainly focused on.
Turk and Trixie. He called me Trixie once when we were humping*

in his sleeping bag. And one day . . . well, it's always day there . . . until it's always night . . . he's filming this great shot of Turk frolicking in the snow. Perfect light. Perfect snow. Real cute frolicking. It was one of the last shots we needed. And suddenly there's Silver Tail—we never really gave her a name—and she presents, and Old Turk had zero qualms about . . .

At just that moment Dr. Salyer entered, and Miriam jumped. "I was about to come tell you!"

He gestured as if to push her vibes back down toward the floor. "I'm impressed with your dedication. Believe me." He pulled the patient's gown aside and listened to her heart. This was not something Miriam had ever seen him do. The stethoscope usually stayed around his neck with his hemp necklace.

"Do you hear something?" said Miriam, when she could stand no more suspense.

"Something," Salyer shrugged. "Just don't know what. Before I walked in, was she agitated?"

Miriam rearranged the gown to conceal Lady Voice's small bare breast. "She . . ."

It's so hard to find places to fuck when you're in high school. So if you somehow find a room, a bed . . . it's so far-fetched, it's like a miracle.

"Huh." Salyer pondered. "I was thinking about what you said. Writing about her."

"You should!"

Up against the grease dumpster behind Dairy Queen . . . ha!

Miriam looked suddenly at the ground, burning with shock in a way she did not when she and the Lady were alone. She could not look at Dr. Salyer as he patted her shoulder on his way out, but the pressure of his handprint remained.

How badly I wanted to tell people! Oh, I knew I wasn't supposed to and I didn't . . . no, I didn't. It's for boys to tell the stories. I wanted a badge. A red letter. A new beauty mark. A gap in my teeth. Or at least some glow. Maybe I did glow a little. I think Brian saw that.

Brian. Crap. I wasn't supposed to say the name. Are you there? Anybody home? Just kidding, of course.

So "Brian" was the poisoner. Now Miriam only had to wait for the story.

"I'm giving her something to help her sleep," said Dr. Salyer. "You look like you could use a break."

⚛

This time she called from her home phone. This time Matt answered. In the background, a child shrieked that it was her turn. Miriam's sister declared that it was nobody's turn. "Uh, hello?" Matt repeated. Miriam felt heat in all the untouched parts of her body, and also in the shoulder where Dr. Salyer had put his hand. "Nooooo!" cried the thwarted child. "Mr. Nobody, I guess," said Matt jovially, and then hung up the phone.

She could not start that all again. That night she could not sleep, wondering if Matt were also awake, if the mystery of the phone call would keep him up. It could not be long before he realized.

⚛

Lady Voice was restless through Miriam's lunch break. Sometimes she went whole minutes with her lips twisting, her blind eyes roving, searching for more words. Finally:

If this is hell, she said with a forced steadiness, *then I am so incredibly sorry.*

While Miriam spooned lentils from her Tupperware, Lady Voice enumerated the regrets that might have landed her in perdition.

I said I couldn't help falling for him, but that wasn't true. I fell intentionally. Threw myself. I was at an age when a young woman wants to be in love and I'd followed my sister in every other way. Plus, I could only be aggressive, physically aggressive, under particular circumstances. I had to have a room close by. Those car rides with the gear shift between you. The pretense of offering a drink . . . I couldn't stand all that. Secondly, I had to be drunk.

So it happened quite naturally on Christmas Eve at my parents' house. He was up late, putting together pink bicycles for the girls, and Libby had gone to bed. There had been a lot of wine with dinner. And so . . . in my childhood bed, where I'd dreamed up my sex life in the first place. And then the next morning we watched the girls pedal around the driveway in their pajamas and for once I didn't have that panicky feeling that everyone had moved on without me. I knew what was under his robe. I knew how the bikes were put together.

Miriam found herself nodding. It was a very difficult thing to have a sister who always seemed to do things first in a way that precluded one from ever doing them as well, especially when she married the only man who could ever suit you.

Oh, God, what if my sister is with me. Libby? You are here. You would be. I mean, to hear all that. Listen, Libby, there are two sides to every seduction story and the woman's is always the most truthful. Men get too addled by their hormones.

"We are both in love with our sisters' husbands," said Miriam. It felt good to say aloud what she had faced only elliptically in her own head. Of course, this admission did not stop Lady Voice from going on.

Men can tell you what happened after, but it's women who remember what came before. Brian was only clear-headed after he blew his load. And that was right when I got dreamy. So yes, after the fact, I may have done a few things that were not wholly logical.

"I'm supposed to be checking my other patients," said Miriam, her voice steady but the words in her head pounding: Brian, Brian, Brian. The poisoner. Lady Voice and the sister's husband had fallen in love and he had poisoned her rather than accept the happiness they might have shared.

Unless the sister had done it.

As she rounded, Miriam thought about the lemmings. When the documentarian was still trying to seduce Lady Voice, when she hadn't yet given in, he'd let her go off with his camera to try and capture a lemming stampede. It had never been done before: *The Magical World of Disney* had faked their footage using an accelerating turntable to fling them over a cliff chosen for its arctic splendor. But Lady Voice had discovered what really happened with the creatures. She caught the lemmings having a sort of orgy, and in the frenzy of rodent partner swapping and frantic haunch-grabbing, a kind of riot had broken out and some lemmings had been shoved or else fell over a precipice. They were struggling in the water, their little libidos all washed away, but Lady Voice had not fished them out because a true documentarian does not interfere.

In every room along the facility corridor, the vegetables were fine. Mrs. Bledsoe's face was still. Mrs. Alden was silent. Might always have been silent. Miriam noted the charts and speed-walked to the next. Their bodies were producing waste at the normal rate. Their minds produced nothing.

The lemmings could've been Lady's big breakthrough, but after the thing with Turk the adulterous fox, the filmmaker got drunk and burned all their footage. *I have literally watched my opportunities go up in smoke*, she said. *Don't be like me.*

Though she was on the far end of the facility, Miriam heard the Lady's voice in her head with perfect clarity: *Help.*

She increased her pace to a squeaky-shoe jog, took a short cut through the outdoor courtyard where some of her colleagues were smoking.

"He calls me Pretty Lady."

"He calls Annette that too."

"Um, excuse me."

"Yeah, but he *knows* our *names*. God."

"He called me Gorgeous after I got that monitor fixed on Mrs. Freely."

"Excuse me."

"Jeez, Miriam, where's the fire?"

In violation of policy, Miriam ran the rest of the way to Lady Voice's room, building enough inertia that once she reached the room, she crashed into the bed rails before she could slow herself.

Dr. Salyer was in Lady Voice's bed, his long body stretched out beside hers. He was pulling back the lid from her roiling eyeball with one hand. Her gown was open, and the fingers of his other hand traced the rim of her exposed belly button.

When Miriam crashed into the bed, this hand recoiled like a spider.

They stared at each other, the knowledge between them like a hunk of ice they'd stuck their tongues to.

"What?" he said. "She asked me to!"

"She doesn't know who she is or what she's saying!"

"That's all she knows. Trust me."

"I—"

"Look, you can write this up if you feel like you need to. But I'm telling you, she didn't even *notice*. Stupid me, I thought if I did what she asked she might somehow . . ."

Miriam cleared her throat of a ghost obstruction. "What did she say?"

"Oh, something went wrong in her childhood, something not fair, something she was supposed to have was given away." *Chick stuff*, his expression clearly said, no different from any of them. He lifted the hand he'd been holding and let it drop. "She can't feel, Miriam."

And then he surprised them both by confessing that the recent power blip had been the fault of a liaison he was having with one of the nurses in a utility closet. Kissing so hard her head mashed some circuit breakers. And she wasn't the only one. He knew every sexual position possible in a utility closet. He was sorry, technically.

"And I know you're perfect. You're this virgin goddess of professional ethics and hard work. But the rest of us are mortals, and the mortals around here have a lot of sex. Oh, not like—" He gestured at Lady Voice behind his hand. "I wasn't *actually* going to . . . But she *was* saying these things and I thought how lonely she is in there . . . and, Miriam, to be honest, I'm kind of in need of a hug."

"What was she saying *exactly*?"

"When she . . . ?"

"Yes."

"She said she needed to be touched. She said her mind got

scrambled when she wasn't having regular sex. It's a common issue, Miriam. And she put it in this way that just made total sense to me . . ."

Miriam whispered: "Sometimes she says things she doesn't mean."

"Can I get that hug? I mean, really? It's been a hard day."

Miriam took her post beside Lady Voice, who was describing a salad she'd had at a nice restaurant on a date, one with pomegranate seeds.

"Raincheck, then," said the doctor, and then, after hovering in the door pretending to read Lady Voice's bedsore rotation chart, "We're okay though, right?"

Miriam still whispered. She wanted the Lady to be heard. "I won't tell if you just go away."

⚓

That night, when her sister answered the phone, Miriam spoke.

"My God," said Renee. "It's been forever."

"I want to be sisters again," Miriam lied.

Renee suggested they get pedicures. Miriam hated to have her feet touched, but perhaps the time for human contact had come. Renee talked the whole time, mostly about the kids, but there were glimpses of Matt. He chewed on things. He left mangled coffee stirrers all over the house, said Renee. Look, while digging for her wallet, she had even found one in her purse. So gross. When Renee wasn't looking, Miriam took the jagged red object. One end had been tucked back into the other like the symbol for infinity. Miriam stowed it in her cheek, where her tongue could trace the teethmarks and corners.

Ugh. Fuck me.

Libby, if you're here with the girls, I'm sorry I said fuck, I guess, but I don't know if you can actually understand me or if I have one of those deaf-people voices.

Here's what I'm thinking, Sis. You should be writing this down. This is good stuff, perfect for a book.

I'll dictate the whole thing: I was loved by a trapeze artist. I was loved by a guy in a cover band who was ten years younger than me and looked exactly like Sammy Hagar. I was loved by a doctor. And who loves me now? You. You who are listening.

Of course, you might be Brian. You might have left her. Really, you have to write the ending. I'd call it "Back from the Poison" but only if it's a happy ending. Otherwise, I guess it's a cautionary tale.

Just remember who owns the movie rights to this shit. When the box-office returns are in, give me some plastic surgery and prop me on the beach. Get me a handsome young guy to put on my sunblock, preferably gay. No, definitely gay. I don't want anyone to get off on washing me.

This notion seemed to depress her. She said nothing for the remainder of Miriam's shift. So when Miriam returned in her street clothes, she herself began to talk, to tell a story of her own childhood. "We went to this church," said Miriam. "The man who would marry my sister went there too, only then he was a boy my sister's age. She didn't notice him when we were kids, not until we were older, so I knew him first. We were volunteers at the Vacation Bible School. When I was twelve, I had a craft booth where the kids could make God's eyes out of yarn and popsicle sticks. His activity was at the other end of the gym, teaching kids to shoot baskets. It was more popular. When he got a break he came over and flicked one of the God's eyes where it hung, then watched it spin. 'What are they?' he said. And even though he was handsome and athletic and followed by several adoring children, he was really asking. The question was sincere."

"God's eyes," Miriam had said, though she wasn't able to explain why. They were just yarn woven into a diamond shape, more like the eye of a cat or a lizard than a sentient being. When you hung them they twisted back and forth on the room's imperceptible air currents, scanning the room but not seeming to see anything. Still, he declared them "neat" and brought the children following him into her booth. Maybe he had felt sorry for her, setting up that booth, trying to teach something no one wanted to learn, but it hadn't felt like pity. No older boy had ever spoken kindly to her before. Ten years later, her sister met him in a bar, totally oblivious that he'd been in her orbit all along. Throughout their courtship, Miriam waited patiently for him to mention the God's eyes, and he never did, not directly, but one Easter when they were decorating eggs, he'd handed her the glitter and said, "Here, Miriam, You're artsy, right?" So she knew he remembered.

Sometimes I wonder if I have a roommate, interrupted Lady Voice.

"Yes," said Miriam. "Something like that."

Maybe I'm lying here talking to some poor sap in a coma. They say it's good for them to be talked to . . . so I would be of some use, at least. I'd like to do something worthwhile.

"My sister has him really well trained," said Miriam. "Like a dog. And he's loyal like a dog, too. But underneath he knows how thin her caring is. He knows that I'm the one who runs deep."

If you're taking dictation, Whoever, you could go on all the morning shows and sell this. It would have such a high pity factor it wouldn't even have to be good. The woman who slept with her sister's husband. That's the big thing, I guess. But somehow it doesn't feel like my fault. It was just one thing happening. Then another. Then this. Lady Voice paused in her reflections.

"It's my turn to confess," said Miriam. "I have a Christmas Eve story too. Matt and I went to a church service. Chelsea was a baby, so Renee stayed home with her. The sanctuary was dark except for candles, and everyone sang 'Silent Night.' The organ stopped playing and it was all just voices. Suddenly there were these tears rolling down my cheeks. Matt looked around for a handkerchief but he didn't have one, and then he just took my hand. We held hands through every verse, and everyone was feeling so caught up they even sang the first verse again. I left the tears where they were until my face was dry and itched a little. Because tears have salt and when the water part evaporates it pinches just a little bit; you have to be paying attention to notice.

"I never told Renee that I cried or that we held hands," Miriam continued, though that should be obvious from the story. "But just like you, I wanted to. I wanted to shout it out. I knew God saw, but I wanted someone on earth to see it too."

But Lady Voice was back on Brian, who after the initial Christmas Eve tryst was always forcing her head into his lap in linen closets at family gatherings. Brian, who once met her at a motel for thirty minutes of sticky maneuvering before showering and hurrying home. She had tried to luxuriate in the cheap, starchy sheets, to feel herself blossoming into a wanton woman, to waste an afternoon quaffing Diet Coke with Famous Amos miniature cookies from the vending machine, but someone from the front desk had knocked on the door to inform her that Brian had only rented the room for an hour and that time was up.

Something about me he could not live without.

"Please," said Miriam. "The poison. Get to the poison."

But Salyer came in and Miriam couldn't contain herself in front of him.

"Don't move," she said giving him the chair. "Just listen."

☙

On the phone, she interrupted Renee in the middle of a diatribe about leg room on airplanes. Miriam had never flown.

"I have to tell you something."

"Of course, sweetie."

Miriam confessed her feelings for Matt as succinctly as possible.

"Oh, Mir, I knew that," Renee sighed. "Honey, you've just got one of those faces that says everything. I just thought, maybe you had learned to live with it."

☙

Dr. Salyer was still in Lady Voice's room when she got back. He raised his hands to indicate the buckled condition of his pants.

"The poison," said Miriam, "did she say how it was done?"

"Yeah, she did get into that a little."

"And?" Miriam was grabbing him by the lapels. The coat was surprisingly starchy in her hands.

"She, uh, she got rose food at the, what's it, the Home Depot. It came in little pellets. We shouldn't dwell on this stuff, Miriam. Hey, is this a hug?"

"She never said that!"

"Look, Miriam, you're a great worker, but I'm seeing this new therapist about my . . . ."

That note was for Brian, said Lady Voice. *Whoever else read it, trust me, you can't understand. I left it for Brian.*

"Didn't you tell me about the Voice Lady's suicide attempts?" said Dr. Salyer.

"I told you about the jokes."

"I could've sworn you said suicide."

"She didn't say that to me." Miriam looked away when she spoke, in case her face really did say everything. "She never talked about the poison."

Because she rented an apartment, Miriam had never been to the Home Depot. It was surprisingly easy: a friendly teenager showed her to the rose food.

Spread across her palm, the pellets looked like sapphires.

In the coffee would be best. These days everyone drank strong coffee in giant paper cups. Dr. Salyer. Her sister. And the patients, they had tubes and ports. Anything could be poured directly in.

For now, they lined her pocket. A small weight, enough to ward off forgetting.

Libby, you could take care of me. Take me home. I'm no longer a threat. The girls could put makeup on me and braid my hair. And if you had a headache one night, and Brian wanted . . . well, it wouldn't make much difference to anyone now.

I probably wouldn't even know.

And still Lady Voice talked on, her mood bouncing in a different direction.

What I hope for most is that I'm some kind of miracle. That people are coming to listen to me. I see them touching the hem of my dress and leaving little gifts, flowers maybe, and chocolate coins and little homemade dolls. Maybe there is a nun who prays over me, and I will be her ticket to sainthood. God has turned His eye benevolent upon me. Because I was as good as dead and I persist. I am still here. And for those of you who've come to marvel, I wish peace unto you forever and ever.

"It's only me," said Miriam. "I've been keeping you alive." But people who aren't heard, she reflected, are not bound by what they say.

Oh, but I know I really will know. If you come to me in the night, my love. God, I hope I'll know.

Birth Stories

By the time the EMTs arrived, Clea was propped on her ruined towels with the baby on her chest, the pulsing purple cord still running between them. She didn't want to cut it. She'd read studies, not that she could quote them just then, but she snarled at the EMTs like a feral raccoon and they agreed to wrap mother and child up together and carry them out on one stretcher. When she got the bill for two ambulance rides (really!), Clea used the fact of live cord to dispute the charge. *We were one,* she hissed into her phone at the customer service rep, head turned toward the shoulder that did not hold a sleeping Amaryllis. *She was plugged in like a damn cell phone.*

We all like Clea.

Monica hosted the potlucks at her apartment, once a month or more. They were a godsend. You can't imagine how we longed for one another's company, even though motherhood had rusted our conversational mechanism to the point where it was not unpleasant just to compare methods of combating diaper rash. Most of us had advanced degrees. This was New Haven.

Monica was on her third child, and she knew best of all what we needed. She put out wine and plastic tumblers, a large bowl of rotini in oily walnut pesto. We all brought what we had time to grab: store-bought pies, cheeses, a half bag of clementines. The events of the day were discussed, of course, but some configuration of the women always ended up on the second-floor porch that overlooked the neighborhood, telling birth stories.

Jill had the hospital play the theme from *Rocky* in the delivery room. The nurse gave her a high-five moments before Easton emerged.

Weston was stubbornly breech, and Paula would swim to the bottom of the pool at the JCC and hold onto the grate for as long as she could, hoping to convince him that down was up. The silence of the deep end was a roar, and she found herself praying, though she had never been to church.

When Paula told us about the underwater prayers we snuck a look at Casey, the downstairs neighbor Monica had gathered into the fold. She seemed so young to be married. Her husband was in a graduate program and her days seemed whimsically open. She'd taken on some babysitting around the neighborhood, was reportedly great with Monica's small wild things.

When Casey went to the kitchen for more pie, Monica lowered her voice reverentially and announced that Casey had "pulled the goalie," that she was *trying*. We all expressed approval: motherhood was the gravitational center of this group. But most of us were not imagining children when we were her age. Perhaps she was religious. Perhaps she would like Paula best. Casey had that kind of beauty that made you long for her friendship, the kind of maddening niceness that made you hope she would choose you.

Lisa got teary after a tumbler of wine: "I feel like I didn't *have* my baby." And she hadn't. They had put up a curtain to hide her body from her, sliced her open, set aside her guts, and pulled the baby out themselves.

Worse: her husband had peeked around the curtain and seen her guts.

I hadn't told them much about how I had Philip. I was saving it, polishing it really, because I fancied myself a writer. I wanted to prove that something profound had happened to me as I'd waited for this baby, my only but not my first. I wanted it to mean as much to the others as it did to me. I'd tried to put the experience in a poem but it wasn't there yet.

It's like that at the widow group, said my grandmother. *I sit through all these stories of men I don't care about. Then I get to talk about Henry.*

It's not like that at all, I said. When I held baby Victoria, I lifted her head to my nose as if inhaling my own daughter. We were all in this together.

⚘

Violet had been so inspired by the birth of Victoria that she quit volunteering in galleries and declared herself a doula. She had a surprising number of clients. This meant she had the most stories. They were all the same story really: the doctor was being ridiculous and she stood up for the mother. *This is her birth*, she would say, *and we are doing it her way*. On the walk home, my husband said, "Technically, isn't it the baby's birth?" Smiling for him felt treacherous.

We weren't always a unit, not like a sitcom where six friends combine in predictable pairings. Monica's and Violet's families went camping together, just them. Clea had yoga friends we never met. A couple of times a year, Jill and I would go for a martini (two at the very most) and rip everyone apart like a couple of momsy Dorothy Parkers. But the potlucks were undeniably our core. We were far from the places and people that raised us. We needed structure and ritual. We needed to understand the dislocations we'd experienced.

When Casey was seven or eight months along, Monica hosted a women-only potluck, an embarrassment of sweets: homemade fudge, ice cream from the best place. A sack of gummi worms.

Casey lay on Monica's vast estate-sale table, naked belly at the center where the Thanksgiving turkey would go. As we recited the things we had learned, we lay strips of papier-mâché over her convexity. A neighborhood tradition: we all had a cast of our fecund bellies hanging somewhere in our homes. Some included the breasts.

Casey was so beautiful with her golden hair fanned out around her glowing face. Unflappable. And some of us were trying to flap her a bit with our stories: the pain, the indignity of Yale being a teaching hospital, the uncontrollable emptying of the bowel (but how casual the nurse was as she changed the paper mat beneath you—*Let's get a fresh one, hon,* as though it hardly mattered). Casey closed her eyes and smiled. It was this peace she brought to babysitting Monica's children, who were wilder every year: we dreaded them in our homes even as we complimented her on their feisty spirits.

Your heart on the outside, we said.

Blood and feces and vomit, we said.

But baby effusions, they were really just slightly processed milk. Like ricotta.

"Hold still until it dries." And she held very still. At one point she may have drifted off to sleep on the haze of our happy horror stories. But a child, I was sure, could destroy even this level of peace. This destruction, we hope, is the start of something new.

In the background, there was a mechanical sucking sound: wuh-whirr, wuh-whirr. This was Françoise. Under her sweater she was harnessed to a pump. Her Micah was adopted and she hoped to bring in milk for him. (It! Is! Possible! According to the League). So far it was only her eyes that leaked. She listened to our stories so earnestly, the only girl at the lunch table not invited to the slumber party, the one who thinks that being herself will get their attention.

We had the names down to Dahlia and Cedar and Amaryllis, Clea told us. *Had to be something from the natural world: she was conceived on a hike. Sometimes I feel like Dahlia and Cedar are still out there, waiting for me to summon them. But I never seem to want sex. Or hiking.*

Few of us could resist giving a full exegesis of our carefully chosen names. We liked literary and historical resonance. We dreaded the commonplace. We theorized what high school bullies would do with the raw material of these names; we imagined what they'd sound like in a history book, a profile in the *Times,* an obituary. These names would survive us when we weren't around to tell the story of their birth. These names were the portion of destiny we got to choose.

☙

Skin to skin was the big thing, we said. We were painting Casey's cast now: suns and stars and a tree growing from a heart. You had to make sure the doctor knew you wanted skin to skin, we said. Put that slimy baby right on my chest. Oh, they usually wiped it off first. Weighed it. Made sure it was breathing. You couldn't blame them for that. But you did. Precious seconds were lost and by the time you could reconnect with the baby it had already been given a score.

We laughed at how it was in movies. An actress with a basketball suddenly leaking water, screaming a few expletives, and boom: an actor baby, several months old and smeared with strawberry jam. It's never fast. Once labor starts, time stretches, stops, doubles back. Refuses to align into the five-minute intervals you promised your doctor you'd wait for before you called.

The most useful thing the midwife said was not to shut our eyes at the height of the contraction. *You'll only close yourself in with the pain.*

When Leticia's contractions hit, she looked wildly around the room for something to read: labels, signs, the spines of medical texts. Then she read them backward because it required more focus. Gave herself a kind of postpartum dyslexia, she told us, laughing. Couldn't anymore see "alert" without thinking "trela." When she saw an exit sign she almost heard a voice whisper "tixe." It rhymed with pixie.

Monica gave Casey a baby necklace of magic stones to relieve teething pain. Some of us would roll our eyes together later, but remained solemn as the homeopathic properties were described.

Everyone was doing things wrong with birth and babies. But our friends were the ones doing the fewest wrong things.

⚘

Cora (easily confused with Clea, but you mustn't) was angry they forgot to offer her the mirror. We'd all been offered the mirror when the crowning began. *Hell, yeah, I wanted the mirror. The freaking interns get the show and not me?*

Casey still had a month to go, six weeks by some calculations, when she abandoned a mug of tea on the porch rail and drove herself to the hospital. Violet got the first text and rushed to meet her. Clea watched Violet's kids. Casey's husband was too deep in the stacks for cell phone reception, so it was Violet who rushed in bearing love, who was pushed from the bedside by an aggressive neonatologist, was hissed at by the expert's pet nurses like rival geese. Violet expected to relay all this to us later; this was how her stories usually went right before their happy ending. Instead, she sent us erratic texts from that one corridor of the hospital that has reception.

Monica was the one who called me with the real news: Casey's baby would not come home to the apartment downstairs with its borrowed bassinet. Was cold. Was blue. Was maybe already incinerated into a pile of ashes with no clear place to rest.

What is there to say? It's the kind of thing that makes empathy seem like a morbid little game.

Casey stayed in bed for a week or so. Monica linked us all to an app that assigned meals. It was both embarrassing and reassuring to deliver these vats of pasta, because she had to leave her bed to meet us at the door. She stood there in her nightgown and offered us tea. Her face was like raw dough. Still, she managed a colorless smile for our feeble jokes.

It wasn't long before she was back tending our children. We all had gaps. We all needed coverage. Monica's little ones couldn't be stopped from running downstairs and demanding Casey's attention for one of their dance routines. She came to the potlucks and never made us feel bad by looking unhappy or longing. She had the same pleasant way about her, the old easy laugh. *She's from the Midwest,* we said.

Of course, none of us was *from* New Haven. But we were all enthusiastic adopters of East Coast mores.

Except the Californians. You'd see them in the produce aisle, the avocado pyramid, squeezing one rock-hard fruit after another with impotent disbelief.

Except the Southerners, who still painted their toenails and wore heels.

The Caribbeans complained of cold and bland food.

The Canadians complained of healthcare and litter.

Mariana from Colombia cringed when people said Columbia.

So we all had our things. Time passed. We shared potlucks and grew together. When the election came, we all had the same signs in our yards.

When he was five weeks old I had a vision of his little fat hand in the juicer. My mouth and throat felt how the juice would be. Like a pulpy V-8.

Not all the stories were happy.

But I got help. I told the doctor.

Did they make you take the test?

Oh, of course. I got the high score!

We laughed. A lot of us had had to take the test: do you have this thought and that? The questions measured our potential for lasting harm versus the run-of-the-mill ruination of a child's first months. Your duty was to accept that your life had been ruined. Sometimes this required pills.

Honestly, we were proud of these less flattering stories. We had accepted the destruction of our selves, but we did not have to pretend that nothing had been lost.

Françoise never did lactate. But she learned to accept her imperfection. This is how fairy tales really end: someone must admit that she has come to the end of the tale. It's like claiming a seat in musical chairs. You can still have a moral, but the moral of all stories is compromise. Despite the door the doctors had already put in her belly, Lisa tried to push her second baby out the traditional canal. It didn't work. But this time she didn't cry and say, "I didn't *have* my baby." She was learning an insomniac stupor that passed for Zen.

The neighborhood children multiplied. They stood up and ran different directions. With their burgeoning personalities came alliances that did not always align with parental ones. The time between potlucks stretched. Still, Monica always had a gathering on Election Day and this year was no exception.

There were American flag cookies, and the bolder children ran immediately to the table and snatched them up before anyone could remind them of their manners. There were tears from the smaller children and from Mariana, who'd spent a lot of time pulling clumpy icing into thin red stripes.

My son did not get a cookie. I saw his eyes level with the tabletop, searching through the crumbs, and I felt a peevishness with other people's parenting that I was disinclined to rise above.

Yet. The evening promised history. We were there to celebrate. There were the usual bottles of price-club reds on the buffet table, but behind the desserts waited real champagne, or at least sparkling wine with a double-digit price point. We eyed it greedily, but . . . manners, restraint. Keeping cart and horse in proper order, if just barely. *There will be other cookies*, I told Philip.

So good! Who made this? Heaven! Our mouths were full and our heads already spinning. Children ran everywhere, laughing and crying and catching each other. Their mouths were purpled with frosting.

"I can't eat until we get more results."

"I can't eat at all." This from Casey. We were surprised to find her with us in the kitchen, not off charming our children and steering them away from fatal games. Though the apartment was overheated, she wore her coat. Her face was flushed. *Nervous?*

No, said Casey. *I believe in Ohio.* Where she was from.

Usually, the potlucks were unbeautiful. We professed not to care whether you brought a three-tier pavlova or a plate of brown apple slices carved with a blunt knife. But this party had inspired a frenzy of domestic arts, ironic, I suppose, though the goods were as sweet as any produced by unironic bakers on the other side.

We ate stripes of roast pepper, stars cut from eggplant. Brownies appeared and we seized them two at a time. Our nerves were starving.

Monica passed the time learning to knit. She poured her attainable-goddess energy into an expanding square on her lap, clickety-click. *I'll have to go forever,* she told us. *I haven't learned to bind off. If I stop it'll all unravel.* Imagine the neighborhood asleep beneath a giant child's blanket.

We poured more price-club red. No one was holding back that night. We spread the known facts of the election before us and it was not difficult to arrange them into a story we could believe. These twinkling facts formed a picture far more legible than constellations, so why did we need to read our stars again and again? We'd been doing this for months. How long it had been since we told a birth story.

I feel unwell, said Casey, her face twisted. She just managed a smile before she went out for air, *no, fine, nothing*, but I longed to follow her out. I was thinking of Monica's fine balcony, high in the air over the neighborhood with its matching signs. A perfect place to survey the world before it changed.

Before I could move a shock ran through the room. We turned to the television. They were calling Florida. Cora was from Orlando, and this was when she began to cry. *Melodramatic*, I thought. I filled my cup and made my way toward the door. I have always loved a balcony. The child I did not have was called Juliet.

On my way past the couch, they called Wisconsin and someone's sudden hand gesture upset my drink. I looked away from the TV to the stricken faces. Letitia's eyes moved frantically back and forth; having found no sense in the words as they were arranged on the screen, she was reading them backward.

I grabbed her arm. "Do you remember when Philip was born? And you brought me those cookies with brewer's yeast, and we had a whole conversation when I didn't know my breasts were out?"

Her voice was vague: "You had a c-section."

"I certainly did not," heat in my cheeks, "I pushed for five hours. *After* I'd been in labor for forty-eight. The first time I went to the hospital they sent me home. Trust me, the doctor said, it gets *a lot* worse. I wanted to punch him. Then I get home and I'm on the birthing ball, and I want something stupid to watch, you know? Sometimes you just want something stupid in front of you, like a famous person or a dog. Only the morning show was taken up with news: people shot in a movie theater . . . and I thought, I'm bringing a kid into this world . . ."

She wasn't even fucking listening.

"My God," said Leticia, "Iowa." Tears spilled.

On the porch, Casey was curled up on a lawn chair. Her coat was off. Her belly . . . it was like we'd gone back in time to that other night.

"I'm pregnant," she whispered. Then quickly sucked in air, her eyes shutting her in with the pain. You're not supposed to close your eyes.

"I'm sorry," she said, when it had subsided. "I didn't want to tell you guys."

"I'll call the hospital," I said. "Your midwife? Who should I call?"

"No," she hissed. "It's Braxton-Hicks."

"Like hell," I said, "let me at least get Violet."

She opened her eyes then: "let me be clear: no."

"Where is Todd?"

"Conference."

All of her features suddenly rushed to the middle of her face, compressing her nose. This pain had come far too quickly after the last one.

"I need you to look," said Casey. I realized she was hiking up her skirt. "And tell me nothing's there."

The top of the head between her legs.

"Oh," I said. When it was me, I had refused the mirror.

There was a pop of a champagne cork released inside the apartment and then a fuss: *It's all that's left to drink and I want to get drunk!*

Bad luck, said someone.

Our luck's already gone.

We would be fighting about that bottle of champagne for a long time. The outrage of and at the opener refused to die. The unlucky pop hung over every potluck thereafter, even after Monica taught the rest of us to knit. Even after we learned to find a measure of solace in the final stitch of a hat. We gorged on cookies but the chocolatey cud could not choke out a voice you didn't want to admit was one of your own, your lesser self hissing: *You hate their blowhard husbands and feral brats. You would close your eyes and Dorothy-Gale back to your own past if it hadn't been blown away. If there were any place to feel peace, you would leave them behind.*

&

On the porch that night, Casey shouted a single expletive and propelled the head into the night air. I caught it. Her. She was wet and tethered, but breathing. There was an eternal still-ness, lasting perhaps three or four seconds. I don't know what Casey suffered then, in the seconds before she summoned the courage to look. Those seconds were the first of a year when my own feelings incinerated any phrase in which I tried to contain them.

I think I said: "She's perfect, but she'll freeze out here." Maybe the communication was telepathic. Somehow we got the baby to Casey's chest, skin to skin, put the coat over them. My breath came in clouds but I could not speak. I couldn't run inside to tell the others.

"I don't know your name," Casey said to the tiny alien. "I'm so sorry I don't know your name."

Acknowledgments

"The Dead Girls Show," "Junk Food," and "Only Children" were featured on *Great Jones Street*. "One Car Hooks into the Next and Pulls," © Giangiacomo Feltrinelli Editore Srl and Prada SpA, appears courtesy of Feltrinelli Editore and Prada and was published in *Prada Journal* and *Fraulein*. "Junk Food" first appeared in *Dogwood*. "North of Eden" debuted on *Hobart*. "The Malanesian" was published by *Lady Churchill's Rosebud Wristlet*. "Waiting for the Miracle: Scenes from the New Brochure" appeared in *storySouth* (as "Waiting for the Night Music"). "Birth Stories" originally appeared in the *Masters Review*.

I owe a lot of people. I'm thankful to my Nashville friends who let me be weird (Laura, Whitney, and Heather) and to the University of Virginia ladies who inspire excellence and fun (Allison, Stephanie, Natalie, Claire, and Claire). To Whit, who always believed. To the teachers: Brenda Gideon, Nancy Howell, George Garrett, Cathy Day, Fiona Cheong, and Michael Byers. To the people who were sent to me just when I needed them, like Holly Chase and Angela Mitchell.

I'm thankful for New Haven, a great little city; for Albertus

Acknowledgments

Magnus College, First Presbyterian Church, and the Westville neighborhood (especially the moms).

I'm thankful to everyone at the MFA program at the University of Pittsburgh, particularly the classmates who've helped me laugh through my angst and, above all, to those who still read my drafts (Kara, Ashleigh, Adam, Robert, Robyn, Anthony, and Colin). Thank you to our "Papaw" Chuck Kinder, who read our worst passages back to us in a smarmy voice, who invited us into his home, who was always better-looking than Michael Douglas and more profound than Grady Tripp (and who couldn't have been any of those things without Diane Cecily).

I come from a family that is critical and creative and always supportive. My grandmothers, Alice Ann and Geraldine, filled me with stories. Carolyn Harris furnished my life with books, and Ron Harris taught me not to declare the work done before revision. I'm still writing to entertain my siblings, Charlie and Susan.

And, of course, the biggest thanks goes to my husband, Keith Wallman, my Prince, who took our beloved Ray and Harris to Monkey Joe's so I could have time to write, who always believed, who helps me dance when everyone's watching.

JUNIPER
JUNIPER PRIZE FOR FICTION

This volume is the eighteenth recipient
of the Juniper Prize for Fiction,
established in 2004 by the
University of Massachusetts Press
in collaboration with the
UMass Amherst MFA Program
for Poets and Writers, to be
presented annually for an outstanding
work of literary fiction. Like its sister award,
the Juniper Prize for Poetry established
in 1976, the prize is named in honor
of Robert Francis (1901–1987),
who lived for many years at
Fort Juniper, Amherst, Massachusetts.